My Secret Unicorn

Starlight Surprise

Touching her heels to Twilight's sides,
Lauren rode him down the overgrown path.
As they got nearer, the tree house seemed to
loom up in front of them. Its old grey walls
were covered with green moss and the air
around it seemed still and silent. A shiver ran
down Lauren's spine. It did look kind of
spooky. Her heart started to beat faster. It
couldn't really be haunted, could it?

My Secret Unicorn

Starlight Surprise

Linda Chapman

Illustrated by Biz Hull

PUFFIN

PUFFIN BOOKS

Published by the Penguin Group
Penguin Books Ltd, 80 Strand, London WC2R ORL, England
Penguin Putnam Inc., 375 Hudson Street, New York, New York 10014, USA
Penguin Books Australia Ltd, 250 Camberwell Road, Camberwell, Victoria 3124, Australia
Penguin Books Canada Ltd, 10 Alcorn Avenue, Toronto, Ontario, Canada M4V 3B2
Penguin Books India (P) Ltd, 11 Community Centre, Panchsheel Park,
New Delhi – 110 017, India
Penguin Books (NZ) Ltd, Cnr Rosedale and Airborne Roads, Albany,
Auckland, New Zealand
Penguin Books (South Africa) (Pty) Ltd, 24 Sturdee Avenue,
Rosebank 2196, South Africa

Penguin Books Ltd, Registered Offices: 80 Strand, London WC2R ORL, England

www.penguin.com

First published 2003
Published in this edition 2004
1

Text copyright © Working Partners Ltd, 2003
Illustrations copyright © Biz Hull, 2003
Created by Working Partners Ltd, London W6 0QT
All rights reserved

The moral right of the author and illustrator has been asserted

Set in 14.25/21.5pt Bembo

Made and printed in England by Clays Ltd, St Ives plc

British Library Cataloguing in Publication Data
A CIP catalogue record for this book is available from the British Library

ISBN 0-141-31928-3

To my parents, for everything ✱

✱ ✱

CHAPTER
One

'Faster, Twilight! Faster!' Lauren Foster cried, burying her hands in Twilight's soft mane.

With a whinny, Twilight surged forward. Lauren's light-brown hair blew back behind her and she laughed out loud as Twilight swooped through the night air, the moonlight shining on his silvery horn.

Lauren loved these moments — the secret times when Twilight, her pony, changed into a magical flying unicorn.

'This is fun!' Twilight exclaimed.

'It sure is!' Lauren agreed as the wind whipped her cheeks. Far below, she could see the treetops and farmhouse where she lived with her mum, dad and younger brother, Max. Her family didn't know about Twilight's secret. In fact, right now, they thought she was in the paddock giving Twilight his evening feed. Lauren smiled as she imagined how amazed they would be if they could see her flying through the moonlit sky instead.

Suddenly Twilight pricked up his ears. 'Hey, listen — what's that noise?' he asked.

Lauren heard a frightened bleating
sound.

'It's coming from the woods,' Twilight
decided. 'It sounds like an animal in
trouble.'

'Let's go and see what it is,' Lauren said immediately.

Twilight cantered down among the trees.

As they got lower, Lauren saw a young fawn caught in a thicket of brambles.

'Oh, look!' she cried. 'The poor thing's all tangled up.'

The thorns were caught in the fawn's russet-red coat and a wiry branch had wrapped itself around one of his legs. No matter how the baby deer struggled, he couldn't get free. His mother watched anxiously from nearby. Seeing Twilight landing on the grass, she shied back in panic. The fawn redoubled his efforts to break free, stamping his hooves in terror.

'We *have* to help him,' Lauren said determinedly.

Twilight nodded and approached the fawn. With a quiet whicker, he touched his horn gently against the fawn's neck. In moments, the terror magically ebbed from the deer's eyes. He stopped struggling and stood still.

Lauren dismounted. Ignoring the thorns that grabbed and tore at her bare hands, she crouched down and began to pull the wiry bramble from around the fawn's leg.

'There you are, baby,' she said at last. 'You're free now.'

Twilight lifted his horn from the fawn's neck and used it to sweep aside the brambles. With a snort, the fawn leapt out of the thicket and ran to his mother's side.

The two deer looked at Twilight in astonishment, then bounded away into the forest.

'It doesn't matter that they've seen

you, does it?' Lauren asked Twilight as she picked her way out of the brambles.

Twilight shook his head. 'Most animals know that a unicorn's secret must be kept. It's other people who must never be allowed to find out about me in case they try to use my magic for bad things.'

Lauren put her arm over Twilight's neck. There was a warm glow in her heart. 'I'm glad we were here to help.'

'Me too,' Twilight agreed. He nuzzled her hands. 'But you've hurt yourself,' he said with concern.

Lauren looked at the deep scratches on her hands. She shrugged. 'It was worth it.'

Twilight bent his head and his horn gently touched Lauren's scratches.

Warmth seemed to flood over Lauren's
hands and she gasped. The scratches
tingled sharply for a few seconds and
then all of a sudden the pain disappeared.
Lauren stared. Where the wounds had
been, there were just some faint pink
marks. 'Wow!' she said, looking at
Twilight in amazement. 'I didn't know
you could do that!'

'Me neither,' Twilight said, looking equally surprised.

'It must be unicorn magic,' Lauren said.

Twilight nodded. Unicorns had many magical powers but neither he nor Lauren knew what they all were yet. Ever since Lauren had first changed him into a unicorn they had been finding out what his powers were.

Taking hold of his mane, Lauren swung herself up on to his back. 'We should go home. If I'm gone too long, Mum or Dad will come outside to find out what I'm doing. We mustn't risk them seeing you.'

With one push of his powerful hind

legs, Twilight kicked up into the sky and they headed back to Granger's Farm.

As they landed in Twilight's paddock, Lauren hugged him. 'I'm going to keep you forever,' she told him happily as she dismounted. 'We'll always live here,' she went on, looking around at the fields and outbuildings of her parents' new farm, 'and if I ever have kids, they can learn to ride on you and they'll believe in unicorns too!' But then a worrying thought struck her. 'How . . . how long do unicorns live, Twilight?'

Twilight looked puzzled. 'I'm not sure.' He snorted. 'I don't really know much about being a unicorn. I left the land where I was born when I was a young foal and I haven't met any other unicorns since.'

'We must find out,' Lauren told him.

Twilight looked thoughtful. 'I bet Mrs Fontana would know.'

Lauren nodded. Mrs Fontana was an old lady who owned a second-hand bookshop and the only other person who knew about Twilight. She too had found a unicorn when she was a young girl. When Lauren had first got Twilight, Mrs Fontana had given her a book about unicorns that had contained the spell she needed to turn Twilight into his magical form. 'I'll ask her next time I see her,' Lauren said.

She looked towards the lights of the
farmhouse. They seemed very bright in
the darkness. It was getting late. 'I should
go in,' she said. Giving Twilight a pat, she
said the words that would turn him back
into a pony.

'Twilight Star, Twilight Star,
Twinkling high above so far,
Protect this secret from prying eyes
And return my unicorn to his disguise.
His magical shape is for my eyes only,
Let him be once more a pony.'

There was a purple flash and then
Twilight was standing there – no longer a
unicorn but a rather shaggy thirteen-hand

grey pony.

He lifted his muzzle to her face. Lauren kissed his soft nose. 'See you tomorrow, Twilight,' she whispered. Then she turned and hurried to the house.

CHAPTER

Two

When Lauren went down for breakfast the next morning, she found her mum and Max already up. Her brother was sitting on their mother's knee. Lauren stared. Now that Max was six, he almost never sat on their mum's knee.

'Bad dream,' Mrs Foster mouthed to Lauren over Max's curly dark head.

Lauren nodded understandingly and,

patting Buddy, Max's Bernese mountain dog puppy who was sitting beside the table, she sat down.

'Lauren,' Max said slowly, as Lauren poured herself some cereal. 'Do you believe in ghosts?'

'No,' Lauren said, looking at him in surprise. 'Why?'

'Because there's a tree house by the creek that everyone says is haunted,' Max replied.

Mrs Foster frowned. 'Is this what your bad dream was about, Max?'

Max nodded.

'But, honey,' Mrs Foster said, turning him so she could see his face, 'ghosts don't exist.'

'But Matthew and David say they saw one,' Max said. 'It was white and it floated through the air above the tree house *and* it made noises.' He looked scared.

'Oh, Max,' Mrs Foster said. 'It was probably a bird. They just *thought* it was a ghost.'

'Yeah, Mum's right. There are no such things as ghosts, Max,' Lauren said, backing her mum up.

But Max didn't look convinced.

'Do you want to go for a ride in the woods after school, Lauren?' asked Mel, one of Lauren's friends. They were leaving the classroom at morning break.

'Definitely,' Lauren replied.

Jessica, their other friend, sighed longingly. 'I wish I had my pony. Then I could come too,' she said. Jessica's dad had promised to buy her a pony in the summer holidays, but that was still ages away.

'You can still come,' Lauren said, not wanting Jessica to feel left out. 'Bring your bike and we can swap. You can ride Twilight some of the time while I ride your bike.'

Jessica's face lit up. 'That would be great!'

Just then, three boys from another class came running down the corridor. They barged past, bumping into Jessica so that she stumbled and fell over. 'Hey!' Lauren

called angrily as they ran on, laughing,
not even bothering to stop and see if
Jessica was OK.

'Ow!' Jessica said, picking herself up off the floor.

'Idiots!' Lauren said, staring after the boys.

Mel nodded. 'It was Nick, Dan and Andrew – Nick's the tall one, Dan's the one with the freckles and Andrew's got the curly hair. They're in my cousin Katie's class. She says they're really mean.'

'Well, she's obviously right,' Lauren said. She hadn't come across the three boys before. Her family had only moved into Granger's Farm recently, and she didn't know everyone at her new school yet.

The three girls started talking again about the ride they were going to go on that afternoon. 'It's so hot – we could visit the creek,' Mel suggested.

'Yeah,' Jessica agreed. 'Shadow and Twilight can go in the water – they'll like that.'

Lauren thought about Silver Creek, the small river that wound its way down from the mountains, through the woods, and remembered the conversation over breakfast. 'You'll never guess what Max said this morning,' she told them with a grin. 'He said that there's a tree house near the creek that's haunted!'

To her surprise, Mel and Jessica didn't grin back.

'Yeah, we know,' Mel said seriously.

'It's up a little path away from the

creek,' Jessica said. 'It's totally spooky.'

Lauren stared at them. 'It can't be haunted, surely?'

Mel's shoulder-length curls bounced as she nodded quickly. 'Jen and Sarah went near it a while back and they said they saw a ghost in the trees!'

'Really?' Lauren said, her eyes widening, as she remembered that Max's friends had told him the same thing.

'But there are loads of other trails that lead to the creek,' Jessica said quickly. 'We don't have to go near the tree house.'

Mel shivered. 'I wouldn't go near it if you paid me a hundred dollars.'

'Me neither,' Jessica agreed.

Lauren didn't know what to say. She

didn't believe in ghosts but Mel and
Jessica seemed genuinely scared. What *was*
this tree house like?

After school, Lauren groomed Twilight.
As she worked she told him about the
ride to the creek. 'It will be lovely,' she
said, stopping to wipe her arm across her
hot forehead. 'You'll be able to go into
the water to paddle and drink.'

Twilight nuzzled her shoulder.
Although he couldn't talk back when he
was in his pony form, Lauren knew that
he understood every word she said.

Just then, Max came running down
the path from the house. He seemed to
have forgotten about his nightmare and

was his usual happy, boisterous self. 'Hi, Lauren!' he shouted.

'Where's Buddy?' Lauren asked, surprised to see Max without his puppy.

'Inside,' Max told her, stopping near Twilight and patting him. 'He just wants to lie down. Mum says it's too hot for him outside.'

'Poor Buddy,' Lauren said, thinking of the puppy's thick black fur. 'I bet he wishes he could take his coat off when the weather's like this.'

Max nodded. 'Are you going out for a ride?' he asked.

Lauren nodded. 'I'm going to the creek with Mel and Jessica.'

'Can I come?' Max said.

Lauren hesitated. She really wanted to
go with just her friends, but it wouldn't
be very nice for Max to be stuck at
home on his own.

'*Pleeease*,' Max begged.

'OK,' Lauren agreed. 'You can come
on your bike – if Mum says it's all right.'

'Cool!' Max said. 'I'll go and ask.' He
turned to run back up the path and then
stopped. 'You're not going near that
haunted tree house, are you?' he asked,
suddenly looking anxious.

Lauren saw the worry in his eyes. 'No,
don't worry, we won't,' she said. 'Though
there's nothing to be scared of anyway.
Ghosts don't exist, you know.'

'I bet they do,' Max said.

'Well, I bet they don't,' Lauren said firmly. She took Twilight's bridle off the fence. 'Now, are you going to ask Mum if you can come? Or shall I go without you?'

'Hold on! I'll go and ask!' Max said, turning to run up the path.

A little while later, Lauren, Mel, Jessica and Max made their way down through the shady woods to Silver Creek. Jessica and Max were cycling ahead on their bikes, while Lauren and Mel rode behind. Occasionally, Twilight would touch noses with Mel's dapple-grey pony, Shadow, as they walked. The two ponies were very good friends.

'This is fun,' Lauren said happily to Mel, as they rode along the sandy trail. Mel nodded and Lauren called out, 'Jessica! Wait and we'll swap – you can ride Twilight the rest of the way to the creek.'

'And you can share Shadow with me on the way back,' Mel offered.

Jessica and Max waited for them to catch up.

Lauren halted Twilight. 'Why don't we go down that track?' she said, nodding towards a small overgrown path that headed off the main trail in the direction of the creek. 'It looks like a short cut.'

'It is,' Mel said, 'but we can't go down there. It goes past the tree house.'

Lauren saw Max gulp. She looked
down the shadowy track with its canopy
of overhanging trees and saw a tree house
up in the branches of an oak tree. It was
made of wood and had windows and a
roof. It looked as if it would be a
wonderful place for a den – from inside
you'd be able to see all around. 'It doesn't
look haunted to me,' she said.

'Well, it is,' Jessica said. 'And there's no
way I'm going down there.'

Max started pushing his bike away
from the path. He looked frightened. 'I
don't like it here, Lauren. I think there
are ghosts.'

'There aren't,' Lauren told him.

Twilight stepped towards the path. His

ears were pricked up and Lauren took
courage. If Twilight wasn't scared, then
why should she be? She had an idea.
'Watch,' she said to Max. 'I'm going to
ride to the tree house and back, just to
prove there aren't any ghosts there.'

'Lauren! No!' Mel and Jessica
exclaimed.

Lauren ignored them. Touching her
heels to Twilight's sides, she rode him
down the overgrown path. As they got
nearer, the tree house seemed to loom up
in front of them. Its old grey walls were
covered with green moss and the air
around it seemed still and silent. A shiver
ran down Lauren's spine. It did look kind
of spooky. Her heart started to beat faster.

It couldn't really be haunted, could it?

Seeming to sense her sudden nervousness, Twilight hesitated, his ears flicking back uncertainly.

'Walk on, boy,' Lauren encouraged, but her voice shook slightly. They were very close to the tree house now. She took a deep breath. Just a few more paces and then she'd be able to turn round and Max would see that there was nothing to be frightened of.

'Whooo-aaaaaoooooo.' A low noise suddenly groaned through the quiet air.

CHAPTER

Three

Lauren gasped. Twilight stopped dead. The noise was coming from the tree house!

Suddenly something exploded out of the bushes in front of them.

For a moment, all Lauren could see was Twilight's grey mane and neck as he reared in surprise. Behind her, she heard screams. She cried out in alarm, but as

Twilight landed,
her cry turned to
a gasp of relief.
A cat was
streaking
away through
the trees, its ears
flat and its long brown tail flying out
behind it.

Lauren laughed shakily and patted
Twilight's neck. 'It was just a cat,' she said.
She turned in the saddle. Mel, Jessica and
Max were looking rather sheepish.

'I almost fainted with fright,' Jessica
called, as Lauren rode back towards them.

'Me too,' Mel said. 'I was sure it was a
ghost.'

'It could have been a ghost cat,' Max put in, looking warily into the trees.

'Max,' Lauren said, getting off Twilight, 'how many times do I have to tell you, there are no such things as ghosts!'

But as she held the stirrup so that Jessica could mount, she felt a flicker of doubt. The tree house really had looked very creepy . . . and what about that noise? It hadn't sounded like any animal or bird Lauren had ever heard. Deciding not to say anything about it in case Max got even more scared, Lauren picked up Jessica's bike.

'You were really brave, Lauren,' Max said, looking at her with respect, as they cycled on ahead of Mel and Jessica.

'There wasn't anything to be scared of,' Lauren told him as firmly as she could. As his bike wobbled over a tree root, she caught sight of something blue sticking out of the bag on the back of his bike. 'Is that Donkey?' she said in surprise.

Donkey was Max's oldest stuffed toy. He was a faded dark-blue colour with droopy ears. When Max had been little he had taken Donkey everywhere with him, but in the last year he had started to say that Donkey was babyish. Although, as Mrs Foster had told Lauren, this didn't stop Max from taking Donkey to bed with him each night.

Max looked round and, when he saw

Donkey's leg sticking out of his bike bag, his cheeks turned pink. 'I didn't put him there,' he said defensively. Quickly he stopped and pushed Donkey into the bag. 'Only little kids have cuddly toys.'

Standing up on his pedals, he rode on.

Lauren smiled to herself. Max would never admit it, but she had a feeling that he had brought Donkey along with him just in case they met any ghosts.

They turned down the track that led to the creek. Lauren was warm from cycling and couldn't wait to take her trainers off to wade in the cool water. There were several people there already – some sitting on the grassy banks, others splashing in the sparkling creek.

'Let's go down to the left where it's less busy,' Mel called. They rode to a quiet spot and dismounted from the bikes and ponies.

'Thanks for letting me ride Twilight,'

Jessica said, dismounting. She helped
Lauren run up the stirrups and loosen
Twilight's girth, and then Lauren led
him down to the water.

Twilight walked in up to his knees
and buried his muzzle in the creek. As
he drank the cool, fresh water, Lauren
thought about that evening when they
would go flying through the sky.

After Twilight had been for a paddle,
Lauren led him out of the river and
tied him up to graze with Shadow.
Then she sat down to take her trainers
off. Mel, Jessica and Max were already
down at the water's edge. Leaving her
shoes beside theirs, Lauren went to
join them.

Jessica had brought a ball and they
threw it to one another. Then they took
it in turns to try skimming stones across
the surface of the water.

'This is great,' Max said, turning a
smiling face to Lauren's as he hunted for
a flat stone. Behind them, Twilight
whinnied.

Lauren glanced round, and saw that
the three boys from school who had
knocked Jessica over were standing by the
pile of shoes. They were nudging each
other and laughing. Lauren saw the
tallest, strongest one, Nick, reach down
and pick up the shoes and pass them to
Andrew and Dan. They were going to
take them!

'Hey!' Lauren shouted, starting to run up the slope towards them.

The boys looked up but, seeing that it was just Lauren, they stood their ground.

Lauren came to a panting stop. 'Leave our shoes alone!'

Andrew, a stocky boy with close-cropped, curly blond hair, grinned and dangled one of Lauren's trainers from his hands. 'Seems to me like you'd have a hard time getting home without them,' he smirked.

'Give them back!' Lauren said.

To her relief, she heard Mel, Jessica and Max running up behind her. They had realized what was happening. 'Give us our shoes!' Jessica exclaimed.

'You'd better ask nicely,' Dan taunted her.

'Hey, what's that?' Nick said, his sharp eyes spotting Donkey's head sticking out of Max's bike bag. The toy had half fallen out when Max had thrown his bike on the ground. Nick swooped down and grabbed Donkey, hauling him out and holding him by his tail. 'Look! It's a stuffed toy!'

Lauren stiffened as she saw poor old Donkey dangling from Nick's huge hand. Only the fact that Nick was head and shoulders taller than she was stopped her from throwing herself at him. 'Put him down,' she said through gritted teeth.

'Yours, is he?' Nick said. His eyes swept

across the group. 'Or maybe he's yours?'
he sneered at Max.

'He's not mine,' Max said, his face
flushing crimson.

'Just give him back,' Lauren said.

'Make me,' Nick taunted.

Lauren lost her temper. Running
towards Nick, she grabbed at Donkey.

With a whoop of delight, Nick
whipped Donkey out of her reach and
then charged away. 'Come and get him if
you want him!'

Dropping the shoes as they went,
Andrew and Dan raced after him along
the bank. Lauren sprinted after them, the
sight of Donkey bouncing around in
Nick's fist spurring her on.

Suddenly the boys stopped. 'Still want him?' Nick called.

'Yes!' Lauren panted as she reached them, and then she realized where they were standing. Just behind them, a little way up an overgrown track, was the tree house!

'Go and get him then,' Nick laughed. Lifting his arm, he hurled Donkey towards the trees. Laughing loudly, he and the other two boys ran away along the bank of the creek.

Lauren stared in horror as Donkey went spinning up into the blue sky, turning over and over until he landed in the branches of a tree . . . right next to the creepy old tree house.

CHAPTER

Four

'Donkey!' Max exclaimed, running up behind Lauren.

'Don't worry,' Lauren said quickly. 'We'll get him down.'

Just then, Mel and Jessica reached them. 'We've got all our shoes,' Mel said. She looked up at the tree. 'Oh.'

'Was he a special toy?' Jessica asked, looking at Max.

Max stared at Donkey for a moment and then he shook his head. 'No,' he said, his voice trembling. 'It's just a silly old thing.' Swinging round, he marched away, but not before Lauren had seen the tears springing to his eyes.

'Max,' Lauren said, going after him and stopping him, 'come on. I'll get Donkey down for you.'

'I don't want him,' Max said angrily, pulling away from her, and he ran down to the creek.

'Maybe we could climb the tree and get it,' Jessica said, joining Lauren. 'But it is very high up.'

'It's OK,' Lauren said quickly, catching Jessica's worried look at the tree house.

'Max says it doesn't matter.' But inside
she was thinking, *Tonight Twilight and I can
fly here. We can get Donkey down.* For a
second, an image of the tree house at
night – dark, spooky, surrounded by trees
– filled her mind, but she forced it away.
She'd be fine with Twilight. They could
just swoop down and get Donkey back
and then fly away.

Feeling happier, she smiled at Mel and
Jessica. They were looking concerned.
'Come on,' she said. 'Let's get back to the
ponies.'

That night, while her mum and dad were
watching a film on TV, Lauren went out
to Twilight's paddock and said the spell

that turned him into a unicorn. There
was a bright purple flash and suddenly
Twilight was standing in front of her – a
snow-white unicorn.

'Hello,' he said, nuzzling her. 'Are we
going to go and get Max's toy?' Lauren
had told him all about her plans for
rescuing Donkey while riding back from
Mel's.

'Definitely,' Lauren replied. She had
heard her mum asking where Donkey
was when Max got into bed that
evening. Max had replied that he didn't
know. He had muttered it as if he didn't
care but Lauren was sure that it did
matter. Although he'd never admit it,
she knew Max loved Donkey almost as

much as he loved Buddy.

Grabbing hold of Twilight's mane,
Lauren mounted. 'Let's go.'

Twilight leapt up into the sky.
'Twilight,' Lauren said, 'you don't think
the tree house is really haunted, do you?'

'I don't know,' Twilight replied.

As the darkness closed in around
them, Lauren felt goosebumps prickle her
skin. 'But ghosts don't exist,' she said,
trying to convince herself by speaking
out loud. 'They're just make believe, like
monsters or dragons or . . .' Her voice
trailed off.

Or unicorns, she thought. She
swallowed, her stomach feeling as if it had
just done a loop-the-loop. People said

unicorns didn't exist, but they did, didn't they? What if she was wrong about ghosts?

Just then her thoughts were distracted by the sight of someone walking in the woods below. Lauren stiffened in surprise. Normally they didn't come across anyone at night. 'Careful!' she whispered quickly to Twilight. 'Look!'

Twilight started to swoop upwards but, as he did so, Lauren recognized the figure below.

'Mrs Fontana!' she exclaimed. 'What are you doing here?' she asked as Twilight cantered downwards and landed beside the old lady.

Mrs Fontana's bright blue eyes

twinkled. 'Walking Walter, of course,' she
said. She whistled softly and Walter, her
little black and white terrier dog, came
bounding out from the bushes. Twilight
lowered his head in greeting. Trotting

over to the unicorn, Walter licked
Twilight on the nose and woofed, before
going to sit at Mrs Fontana's side.

'He says it is good to see you,' Mrs
Fontana said. Her face creased into what
seemed like a hundred wrinkles as she
smiled. 'And he's right – it is. What are
you both up to tonight?' she asked.

'We're going to get my brother's toy,'
Lauren replied. 'Some boys threw it up
into a tree.'

Mrs Fontana nodded, looking pleased.
'So, you're still doing good things then?'

Lauren nodded. Ever since she had
turned Twilight into a unicorn, they had
been secretly helping several of her
friends overcome problems – although, of

course, her friends knew nothing about
the magical side of Twilight. That was the
thing about unicorns – they roamed the
human world looking just like little grey
ponies until they found a Unicorn Friend
– a child with enough imagination to
believe in magic. Once the Turning Spell
had been said and the unicorn had
changed into their magical form, then
they and their Unicorn Friend worked
together, helping others.

'That's as it should be,' Mrs Fontana
said. 'My unicorn and I did a lot of good
too.'

'What happened to your unicorn?'
Lauren asked, remembering her own
conversation with Twilight from the night

before. 'Did he . . . did he die?' Her voice faltered on the words as she imagined how she would feel if Twilight ever died. She was relieved when Mrs Fontana smiled.

'Oh no,' the old lady replied. 'He returned to Arcadia – like all unicorns do.'

Lauren and Twilight stared at her, not quite understanding.

'Unicorns come to this world to carry out good deeds,' Mrs Fontana explained. 'Then they go back to Arcadia – the magical world where they were born. Those unicorns who have been the most courageous and resourceful earn the right to become Golden Unicorns, the wise

rulers of Arcadia. That's why you two
have to work out how to use Twilight's
magical powers all by yourselves,' she said.
'It's a test for Twilight – being here. If he
does enough good work, then maybe
he will become a Golden Unicorn
one day.'

Lauren gripped Twilight's mane. He
was going to go away one day? But he
couldn't. He was hers.

Twilight seemed to be thinking the
same thing. He stamped his foot in alarm.
'But I don't want to go back to Arcadia! I
want to stay here with Lauren!'

'One day you will feel differently,' Mrs
Fontana said. 'It is your destiny.' Seeing
the alarm and unhappiness on their faces,

she shook her head in a kindly way. 'Do
not worry about this now. Concentrate
on being here together.' She smiled.

'Now, my dears, I must go. Come, Walter,' she said to the little dog.

Walter leapt to his feet, and he and Mrs Fontana vanished among the trees.

CHAPTER
Five

Silence fell on Lauren and Twilight as they both thought about what it would be like to leave the other.

At last Lauren took a deep, trembling breath. 'We should get Donkey,' she said quietly. 'It's getting late.'

Twilight nodded. Without saying a word, he took off into the sky. But Lauren didn't feel any of the usual joy she

felt when flying. At the back of her mind,
a thought was trying to turn itself into
words. Lauren tried to catch hold of it –
she was sure it was important and that it
had something to do with what Mrs
Fontana had just said.

'We're here,' Twilight announced as
they reached the creek. 'We should get
Max's toy.'

Lauren took a deep breath and agreed.
After all, she and Twilight were supposed
to do good, just as Mrs Fontana had said.
The old lady's words came back to her:
*Unicorns come to this world to carry out good
deeds and then they go back to Arcadia.*

The thought that had been hovering
vaguely in Lauren's mind suddenly

became clear.

'Twilight!' she gasped, as he rose upwards. 'Stop!'

Halfway to the treehouse, Twilight stopped and hovered in the air. 'What is it?'

'Don't you see?' Lauren said. 'The more good we do, the sooner you'll go away.'

'I don't understand,' Twilight said.

'Mrs Fontana said that you were here to pass a test,' Lauren said. 'To pass it you help others with me. That must mean that when we've done enough good deeds, you'll go back to Arcadia.'

Twilight spoke slowly. 'So, you mean the more I help, the sooner the time comes for me to go away?'

'Yes,' Lauren whispered.

There was a long pause.

Lauren looked at Donkey hanging in the tree and bit her lip. 'You know,

maybe Max doesn't really want Donkey
back,' she said suddenly.

He does, a voice inside her head
protested. Lauren tried not to listen to it.

'I mean, he *did* say that he thought
Donkey was babyish,' she went on out
loud, 'and that he didn't want him any
more.'

Her mind filled with a picture of
Max's face when he had first seen
Donkey in the tree. She pushed it away.

'And he's right,' she went on. 'It *is* kind
of babyish for a six-year-old to still take a
cuddly animal to bed.'

'So, you think that maybe we *shouldn't*
get the toy,' Twilight said hesitantly.

'Yes,' Lauren said. A horrid guilty

feeling was welling up inside her, but she ignored it. 'Let's leave Donkey here.'

'Are you sure?' Twilight asked.

'Definitely,' Lauren said. 'Let's go home.'

But inside she was far from sure.

They flew back to Granger's Farm in silence.

'Goodnight,' Lauren said, after she'd changed Twilight back into a pony. 'I'll see you in the morning.'

Twilight nodded, but Lauren was sure his eyes looked troubled.

We've done the right thing, Lauren told herself as she walked back to the house. *Max didn't really want Donkey.*

And you didn't want to do a good deed

with Twilight in case it brought him closer to going away, the little voice in her head said.

'That's not true,' Lauren said aloud, wishing that the little voice would leave her alone.

On the way up to her bedroom, she looked into the lounge where her mum was reading and her dad was watching the TV.

'I'm going up to bed,' she said.

Her dad looked at the clock on the wall. 'Have you been with Twilight all this time?' he asked in surprise.

'Yes,' Lauren replied.

'But it's dark outside,' her mum said. 'What have you been doing?'

Lauren shrugged vaguely. 'Talking to him – this and that.'

Her dad shook his head. 'You know, I thought that maybe you'd lose interest in ponies once you had one of your own, Lauren Foster. But you've sure proved me wrong.'

Her mum smiled. 'You really love that pony, don't you, Lauren?'

Lauren nodded. 'Yes,' she said, 'I do.' She imagined Twilight leaving her and her heart felt as if it was going to break.

Feeling tears spring to her eyes, she rubbed her hand across her face, pretending that she was tired so that her mum and dad wouldn't see. Her mum came over and kissed her. 'You look exhausted, honey. Go and get ready for bed. I'll be up shortly to say goodnight.'

Lauren didn't sleep well that night. She tossed and turned in her bed – one minute thinking about Twilight going away, and the next thinking about Donkey still hanging in the tree.

She woke up early and got dressed. On the way downstairs she passed Max's room. Max wasn't in his bed. Wondering where he was, Lauren carried on. The door to her mum and dad's room was open and when Lauren looked in she saw that Max was in their parents' bed. Her dad had already got up and had

started work on the farm. Lauren
stopped in the doorway.

Mrs Foster opened her eyes. 'Hi, there,'
she said, sitting up in bed. She glanced at
the bedside clock. 'You're up early.'

'I was having bad dreams,' Lauren told
her.

'Not you as well,' Mrs Foster said,
yawning. 'Max had another nightmare last
night too.'

Just then Max woke up. 'Mummy?'

'I'm here,' Mrs Foster said, kissing his
dark head.

'I like sleeping in your bed,' Max said
to her, cuddling closer.

'Well, I'm afraid that tonight it's back
to your own bed,' Mrs Foster said.

'There's hardly any space for your dad
and me with you in here as well.'

'But my bed's lonely,' Max said.

Mrs Foster ruffled his hair. 'It won't be

when we find Donkey. I'll have a look for him today.'

Max's eyes met Lauren's. *So*, she realized, *he hasn't told Mum where Donkey really is.*

'I don't need Donkey,' Max muttered.

'Well, maybe I'll try and find him anyway,' Mrs Foster said, smiling at Lauren.

Max saw the smile and threw the covers back. 'You won't be able to,' he said, getting up. 'And, anyway, it doesn't matter. I told you – I don't care.' But as he pushed past Lauren, she saw the unhappiness in his eyes.

Lauren felt dreadful all day. *I should have*

got Donkey down from the tree for Max, she
thought as she stared unseeingly at a page
of sums at school. It was just . . .

She swallowed as she admitted the
truth. It was just that if she and Twilight
did good deeds, then Twilight would have
to leave her.

Mel leaned over. 'You OK, Lauren?'
she asked.

'I'm fine,' Lauren said, trying to smile.

But inside, she knew that she wasn't
fine at all.

CHAPTER
Six

'I don't want to go to bed,' Max said, clinging to Mrs Foster's arm that evening when she suggested that it was his bedtime. 'Can't I stay up – please, Mum?'

'No,' Mrs Foster said, looking at his pale face. 'You look worn out. Come on – upstairs with you. You can snuggle down in bed and I'll read you a story.'

Max hung back. Mrs Foster crouched
down beside him. 'Hey, how about just
for one night, we let Buddy sleep in your
room with you?' she said. 'Will that make
you feel better?'

Max nodded. 'Yes.'

'OK then,' Mrs Foster said kindly. 'Just this once. Come on, Buddy,' she said to the puppy, who was stretched out on the floor in front of the sofa. 'You can come upstairs.'

Buddy leapt to his feet. Wagging his tail, he bounded towards the door, stopping to give Max a slobbery lick on the way. Looking a bit happier, Max headed for the stairs with Mrs Foster.

Lauren followed them. Sitting down in her room to do her homework, she could hear her mum settling Max in his bed and starting to read to him.

Mrs Foster read on for what seemed a long time. It wasn't until Lauren had started on the last of her homework –

spellings – that she heard her mum turn
the light off and quietly leave Max's
room.

'Mum!' It was Max's voice.

Through her half-open door, Lauren
saw her mum pause in Max's doorway,
her face looking tired. 'Yes, Max?'

'I . . .' Max seemed to be struggling
with the words. 'I want Donkey.'

Lauren's heart clenched.

'I'm sorry, honey,' Mrs Foster said
gently. 'But I just don't know where he
is. Cuddle your other toys instead. We can
have another look in the morning.'

She waited a moment by the door.
When Max said no more, she turned and
went downstairs.

Lauren looked at the printed column
of spellings in her school book with its
red and gold logo, but she couldn't
concentrate on them. After a while, she
went to her brother's bedroom. 'Max?'
she whispered. There was no answer.
Maybe he'd fallen asleep.

Lauren pushed the door open. 'Max?'
she whispered again.

And then she heard the sound of Max
crying quietly.

'Oh, Max!' Lauren exclaimed. She ran
to his bed. Max was lying face down,
crying into his pillow. Buddy was sitting
beside him, whimpering anxiously.
Crouching down, Lauren put her arms
round her little brother. 'Max, please

don't cry.'

Through the darkness, Max lifted a
tear-stained face to hers. 'I miss Donkey,
Lauren.'

The words tumbled out of Lauren. 'I'll

get him for you,' she said.

Max sat up in bed and stroked Buddy's head. 'You can't. He's too high up in that tree and it's right by the haunted tree house.' He gulped and Buddy reached up to lick the salty tears from his cheeks with his pink tongue. 'He's gone forever.'

'He hasn't,' Lauren told him. 'I'll get him. I promise.'

'Really?' Max said, a faint light of hope glimmering in his eyes.

Lauren nodded. 'Really,' she answered.

Leaving Max with Buddy, Lauren went downstairs. 'I'm just going to see Twilight,' she said to her mum and dad, who were in the kitchen.

'Don't be out too long,' her dad said. 'It'll be dark soon.'

'Have you done your homework?' Mrs Foster asked.

Lauren nodded. She still had the spellings to learn but she could look over them the next morning.

'OK then,' her mum said.

Lauren pulled on her trainers and hurried outside. As she reached the path that led to Twilight's paddock, she started to run.

Hearing the sound of her footsteps, Twilight came trotting to the gate.

'Twilight,' Lauren said quickly. 'We've got to go out flying.'

Twilight whinnied and Lauren said the

words of the Turning Spell.

'What's happened?' he asked.

'Max is really upset about Donkey,'
Lauren said. 'He can't sleep. I feel awful.'
She stepped forward and stroked his
neck. 'Twilight, even if it does mean that
it brings the time closer when you have
to go away, we've got to get Donkey
back. I just can't let my brother be so
upset.'

'Of course you can't,' Twilight said.
'We must help.' He shook his mane. 'It
was strange yesterday when we didn't get
Max's toy. It somehow felt wrong. But
this,' he nuzzled her, 'this feels right.'

'I know,' Lauren replied with a smile.

★

They flew to
the creek
and landed
on the
grassy bank.
Donkey was still hanging in
the branches of the tree. It was
getting dark. Lauren's eyes moved to the
nearby tree house. It looked shadowy and
menacing in the gloom. She remembered
the noise she had heard as she had ridden
up to it the day before and suddenly she
felt afraid. What if it really was haunted?
She and Twilight were going to have to
fly right beside it to get Donkey.

Trying not to feel scared, Lauren
patted Twilight's neck. 'OK,' she

whispered. 'Let's fly up.'

Twilight leapt upwards. Lauren's heart
was pounding but she felt strong – she
knew she was doing the right thing. As
Twilight reached the branches where
Donkey was hanging, he stopped and
hovered in the air. Untangling Donkey's
woolly mane and tail from the branches,
Lauren took him safely into her arms.

'I've got him!' she cried.

Twilight flew on upwards. As they rose
up past the tree house, Lauren even felt
brave enough to look in through the
windows. The moon was shining
through one of them, lighting up the
inside of the wooden house. There was
nothing there. It was empty. Well, apart

from some rubbish on the wooden
floorboards – chocolate wrappers, empty
cans, a comic and a . . .

'Twilight – stop,' Lauren said suddenly.

'What's the matter?' Twilight asked.

'Can you take me close to one of the
windows, please?' Lauren asked.

'Sure.' Twilight did as she asked. Lauren
looked in again. Yes, there on the floor of
the tree house was a school spelling book
with a red and gold logo. It was from
Lauren's school! But what was it doing in
the tree house?

She also realized that the rubbish on
the floor looked new. The discarded
wrappers were still bright and colourful
and the comic was the latest issue of

Spider-man – Lauren had seen some of
the kids in her class reading similar copies
only the day before.

But who would have been in the tree
house? Everyone was scared of it.

Lauren looked at the spelling book
again and made up her mind. 'I have to
go inside,' she said to Twilight.

'OK,' Twilight said, flying as close to
the window as he could.

The wood of the tree house was old
but solid. As Lauren grabbed hold of the
window sill and pulled herself over it,
she found herself thinking again that it
would make a wonderful den. It was so
lovely up in the tree and in the daytime
you must be able to see all around.

She saw something white in one corner and stopped. It looked like a pile of cotton sheets. Her skin prickled. What if there was something under them?

Taking a deep breath, she crept over and touched the edge of the sheet with the toe of her trainer. Nothing moved. Lauren moved the top sheet. Underneath it there were two more sheets, a toy microphone and a long stick.

Lauren frowned and picked up the microphone. Max had one like it at home. It made your voice sound strange and echoey when you spoke into it. But what was it doing here?

She walked over to the school book and opened it curiously. Who did it belong to?

A name was written inside.

Lauren gasped. *Nick Snyder.* He was the

boy who had thrown Donkey into the

tree. But what had he been doing in the

tree house?

Her eyes widened. There was only one explanation. 'Twilight,' she said, hurrying to the window. 'I think the boys who threw Donkey into the tree are trying to pretend the place is haunted!'

'What?' Twilight snorted in surprise.

'There's a school book on the floor that belongs to one of them,' Lauren told him quickly. 'So they must have been here. There are some sheets and a stick. You could hang the sheets on a stick and wave them high up in the branches to make people think they've seen ghosts. There's also a toy microphone. I bet the boys have been using it to make that spooky noise we heard.'

'But why would they do that?'

Twilight asked in astonishment.

'I don't know,' Lauren said. She started to climb over the window ledge and on to his back. 'But I think we should try to find out.'

CHAPTER

Seven

As Lauren went up to her bedroom, she stopped by Max's door. 'Max,' she said softly.

There was only the sound of Max's breathing. He had finally fallen asleep.

Lauren went quietly into the room. Buddy was lying beside the bed. He thumped his tail on the floor when he saw Lauren, but he didn't get up.

Lauren tucked Donkey under Max's arm. ''Night, Buddy,' she whispered and then, with a smile, she crept out of the room.

At six o'clock in the morning, Max came flying into her room with Donkey in his arms. 'Lauren!' he cried, jumping on to her bed and waking her with a start. 'You got Donkey back for me!'

Lauren grinned. 'I told you I would.'

'But how?' Max said.

Lauren decided it was best to tell him part of the truth. She lowered her voice. 'I used magic,' she whispered.

Max didn't quite seem able to decide whether to believe her. 'Really?'

Lauren nodded.

'Wow!' Max gasped, his eyes widening.

'But you can't tell anyone,' Lauren whispered quickly. 'If Mum asks where Donkey was, just tell her that you found him under the bed or something.'

'OK,' Max agreed eagerly. He sat down on the bed. 'What sort of magic was it, Lauren?'

'I can't tell you,' Lauren smiled. 'It's a secret kind of magic.'

'Please tell me,' Max begged.

Lauren shook her head.

'But . . .'

'Max!' Lauren exclaimed and, picking up one of the cuddly toys from the end of her bed, she hit him with it. 'I said it's a secret!'

Max hit her back with Donkey and the next minute they were in the middle of a toy fight, gasping with laughter as they fell about on Lauren's bed.

At school that day, Lauren watched Nick and his friends. During break they hung out together, muscling in on a game that some of the younger kids were playing.

Lauren frowned as she watched them. They were so mean.

As she and her mum and Max drove home from school that afternoon, Lauren saw Nick and his friends cycling along the pavement. They were pedalling fast, weaving in and out through the other

children. As Lauren watched, they turned
down a path that led in the direction of
the creek. *And,* Lauren thought, *towards
the tree house.*

As soon as Lauren got home, she
groomed and saddled Twilight. 'We have
to go to the tree house,' she told him. 'I
want to see if Nick and his friends are
there. But they mustn't see us.'

As they set off into the woods,
Twilight pulled eagerly at his bit and
Lauren let him trot along the sandy trail.
As she rode, she wondered how she could
get close to the tree house without the
boys seeing.

Suddenly Twilight stopped. He was
looking down a little overgrown path to

the right, as if he wanted to go that way.

'No, Twilight,' Lauren said. 'We're going to the tree house.'

Twilight stamped his foot.

Lauren frowned. Was he trying to tell her something?

'You think we should go down here? Does this lead to the tree house?'

Twilight nodded.

Lauren touched her heels to his sides and he walked quickly down the path. After a little way, it forked. Lauren left the reins loose on Twilight's neck and he took the right-hand path. They walked on for a minute more, with Lauren dodging the low overhanging branches. Then Twilight came to a halt.

Looking straight ahead, he whickered softly.

Lauren stared. The tree house was just ahead of them, half hidden by trees. If she got off and crawled through the undergrowth she could get to it without having to go down one of the main paths – she could see what the boys were doing without being noticed.

'Clever boy,' she breathed, giving Twilight a hug.

Twilight snorted. Lauren dismounted and began to creep through the thick green undergrowth towards the tree house.

As she got closer she could hear the sound of low voices. Her heart started to thump loudly in her chest. What if the boys saw her? What would they do? She pressed on, trying to ignore the fact that the palms of her hands were starting to sweat.

'It's going to be so cool, staying here tonight,' she heard one of the boys say. *Andrew*, she thought.

Stopping, she crouched behind a bush and listened hard.

'Really cool,' she heard Nick reply. 'We can bring food with us and have a midnight feast.'

Dan laughed. 'Can you imagine how scared everyone else at school would be of staying here overnight?'

'They are so sure it's haunted,'

Andrew said.

'Hey, I hear somebody coming!' Dan said suddenly. 'On the left.'

Lauren froze as for one horrible moment she thought they meant her. But then to her relief she heard the sound of them moving to the far side of the tree house.

'Two girls,' she heard Andrew say.

Nick laughed. 'Come on, guys, into positions.'

Lauren peered out from round the bush. She could just make out two girls, who looked about seven years old, walking rather nervously along the trail that led from the creek past the tree house.

'Go on – I dare you to touch the tree,'
one of them said to the other.

'Sure,' she heard the other reply rather
nervously. 'But it's not really haunted.'

And then, seemingly from the air,
came a disembodied groaning noise.
Lauren knew exactly what was making
the noise – one of the boys with the toy

microphone. She could have laughed out loud at how simple it was, but it wasn't funny.

The two girls screamed and raced back to the creek.

From the tree house came the muffled sounds of laughter.

'That was great!' Lauren heard Dan say.

'They were so scared,' Nick said. 'It's perfect. If I hadn't thought of this, then we'd have had to share this place.'

He sounded very pleased with himself and Lauren felt a wave of anger. Little kids were having nightmares about ghosts and it was all because three boys were too selfish to share the tree house. It was only the thought that

the three of them were so much bigger
than she was that stopped her from
climbing up there and telling them what
she thought of them.

Instead, she crawled back to Twilight.

She didn't say anything until they had
moved out of sight of the tree house, and
then she told him what she had heard.

'Can you believe them?' she demanded
indignantly. 'Of all the dumb things to
do!' Twilight shook his head. Lauren
longed for him to be able to answer back
but she couldn't risk turning him into a
unicorn in broad daylight in case
someone saw. Instead, she stroked his
neck. 'We've got to do something about
them.'

She thought hard. The question was —
what?

After supper, Lauren left the house and,
in the gathering dusk, turned Twilight
into a unicorn.

'What are we going to do about those
boys?' Twilight said immediately.

'I don't know,' Lauren said. She'd been
wracking her brains.

'We should scare them just like they've
been scaring everyone else,' Twilight said.

'But how?' Lauren asked.

'I'm not sure,' Twilight admitted with a
snort.

Lauren remembered a bit of the boys'
conversation. 'They said they were going

to stay at the tree house tonight. Let's go there now. Maybe we could make noises in the bushes or something – that might scare them.' She wasn't convinced it would work but she desperately wanted to do something, and fast.

Twilight nodded. Lauren climbed on to his back and they cantered away into the sky.

To Lauren's surprise, the tree house was quiet when they arrived. 'They're not here yet,' she said.

'Listen,' Twilight said. 'They're coming.'

Lauren heard the sound of the boys running along the path from the creek.

'Let's fly higher!' she said quickly.

'They mustn't see us.'

As Twilight rose into the sky, Nick and Andrew came running along the path. They were clutching several bags of sweets and bars of chocolate. Dan was a little way behind, carrying a large bag of drinks cans.

'Wait!' he was saying. 'These drinks are heavy!'

'Come on!' Nick called to Andrew. 'Let's eat everything before Dan gets here!' He shouted it loud enough for Dan to hear.

'Hey!' Dan shouted in protest. 'Wait! That's not fair!'

Nick and Andrew reached the rope ladder. Nick climbed into the tree house

first while Andrew waited. Then Andrew
passed the food and scrambled up the
ladder himself.

Watching from above, Lauren saw

Nick whisper something to Andrew. They
both grinned and started to haul up the
ladder.

The last rung had just disappeared into
the tree house when Dan came panting
up the path. 'Put the ladder back down!'

Nick and Andrew looked out,
grinning. 'Not till we've eaten all the
food!' Nick said.

Then he and Andrew disappeared back
into the tree house.

Dan shouted out angrily. 'Come on,
guys. Stop messing around. Let me in!'

Neither Nick nor Andrew appeared
and it seemed as if they were going to eat
all the chocolate and crisps themselves.

Dan looked around. It was getting

darker by the second and Lauren saw an
alarmed expression cross his face. An owl
hooted overhead and she saw him jump.
'This isn't funny any more,' he shouted
up to the boys in the tree house. 'Let
me in.'

Nick's voice floated out through the
windows. 'Scared of the ghosts?' he called.
And he and Andrew cracked up laughing.

His words gave Lauren an idea.
'Twilight! This is our chance!' she said.
'Let's swoop down and frighten Dan.
Make yourself look fierce – point your
horn at him.'

'You mean, let him see me?' Twilight
said in astonishment.

'It's dark. He's alone. No one will

believe him if he says he's seen a
unicorn.' Lauren knew it was risky but
she had a feeling it would work. If they
could frighten Dan, then maybe they
could frighten the other two as well.
'Come on!' she said, grabbing his mane.
'Let's go for it!'

CHAPTER

Eight

With a great whinny, Twilight plunged down from the sky. He galloped through the air towards Dan, his horn pointing at the boy, his dark eyes flashing with fire.

Lauren ducked low on Twilight's back but not before she had caught sight of Dan staring at Twilight in horror. His mouth gaped open.

'*Arghhhhhhhh!*' he yelled in terror, as
Twilight bore down on him.

The unicorn swooped upwards,
missing him by centimetres, and
disappeared into the darkness of the
woods. He landed quietly.

Dan was still yelling and now the

other boys were shouting too. There was
the sound of the rope ladder being let
down. Lauren clutched Twilight's neck,
gulping back her laughter as she
remembered Dan's horrified face when he
had seen Twilight appear out of the sky.

'What's up?' she heard Nick shouting
to Dan as he clambered down the ladder.

'It was . . . it came through the sky at
me . . . big horn . . . galloping!' Dan
shouted.

'What came at you?' Lauren heard
Andrew demand.

'It was a uni– ' Dan broke off as if he
couldn't believe what he had seen with
his own eyes. 'It was a horse,' he said
quickly. 'A great white flying horse.'

'A flying horse!' Nick and Andrew exclaimed.

'With someone riding it,' Dan gasped. 'It came out of the sky. It just galloped straight at me. I couldn't see the person's head. Just their legs.'

'You mean a headless horseman?' Andrew laughed. 'Like a ghost!'

'Yeah!' Dan said, agreeing quickly. 'Yeah, that's what it was – it was a ghost!'

Nick and Andrew both laughed loudly.

'As if,' Nick said.

An idea filled Lauren's mind. 'Gallop round!' she said to Twilight. 'Make the sound of hoofbeats. Let's make them think there really *is* a headless horseman!'

Twilight didn't need telling twice.

Pricking up his ears, he started to canter through the bushes around the tree house, stamping his feet down as hard as he could.

'Listen!' Dan cried. 'There it is again!'

'Hey, you're right. I can see it!' Nick said, suddenly sounding frightened. 'Look – it's moving through the trees.'

'I can see it too!' cried Andrew.

Whinnying loudly, Twilight started cantering directly for the tree house. The sound of his hoofbeats seemed to fill the forest as he galloped down the path.

'*Arghhhhhhh!*' all three boys shouted in fright. 'It's a ghost – a real ghost!' And the next minute, Lauren saw them running off through the woods, falling over tree roots and stumbling over stones in their panic. Still yelling, they disappeared out of sight.

Twilight stopped. 'We did it!'

Lauren's face split in a grin of astonishment and delight. They'd actually scared the boys away.

Twilight tossed his mane proudly. 'I must have looked really frightening.'

'I reckon you did,' Lauren smiled, hugging him. 'You were great.'

'It was your idea,' Twilight said.

'They were so scared,' Lauren laughed. 'Serves them right.'

Twilight snorted in a way that made it sound very much as if he was laughing too. 'Somehow I don't think they'll be coming back here in a hurry.'

Lauren patted his neck. 'I think you're right. Come on, let's go.'

As Twilight rose into the sky, Lauren frowned. 'I wonder if Nick's spelling book is still in the tree house,' she said. 'He'll get into trouble if he goes to school and says he's lost it.'

Part of her thought that Nick Snyder deserved all the trouble he got, but then she told herself not to be mean. He'd had enough of a fright without getting into trouble at school as well. 'Let's find it for him,' she said.

Twilight flew to the window. 'You know,' Lauren said, as she climbed inside to get Nick's book, 'this is going to make a great place for everyone to come and play. Now the boys have left it, everyone will be able to use it.' She reappeared with Nick's school book.

'So it looks like we've done two good deeds, after all,' Twilight said.

Lauren paused on the window ledge. 'I guess we have.'

They looked at each other. Neither of them spoke, but Lauren was sure she knew what Twilight was thinking. Had they just brought the time when he was going to leave her even closer?

The happiness that had been fizzing through her suddenly faded away.

She climbed slowly on to his back and they set off in an unhappy silence.

They were almost back at Granger's Farm when Lauren saw someone in the woods. 'It's Mrs Fontana and

Walter,' she said.

Twilight landed beside the old lady
and the terrier.

'Hello again,' Mrs Fontana said, smiling
at them. 'Where have you two been?'

'We've been at the creek scaring away
some boys who'd been pretending the
tree house was haunted,' Lauren replied
in a subdued voice.

Mrs Fontana noticed her sadness. 'What's
the matter? You don't sound very happy.'

Lauren looked at the ground. Twilight
hung his head.

'What is it?' Mrs Fontana said with
concern.

The words came tumbling out of
Lauren's mouth. 'Oh, Mrs Fontana,' she

answered unhappily, 'I don't know what to do. The more we help people, the sooner Twilight will have to go back to Arcadia. I want to do good but I don't want him to leave.'

'But the amount of good you do doesn't affect when Twilight leaves,' Mrs Fontana said in surprise.

'It doesn't?' Lauren said.

'No, my dear,' Mrs Fontana replied, shaking her head. 'You must have misunderstood me. Twilight will be with you for as long as you want him to be. It's up to you when he leaves.'

'I . . . I don't understand,' Lauren stammered in confusion.

Mrs Fontana took hold of her hands.

'One day, you will grow up and no longer need Twilight, Lauren,' she said, her bright eyes looking into Lauren's face. '*That* will be the day when the time has come for Twilight to go – and if he's done enough good deeds, then he'll become a Golden Unicorn.'

'But I'll always need Twilight,' Lauren exclaimed. Her eyes lit up with hope. 'Does that mean he can stay with me forever, Mrs Fontana?'

'He will stay for as long as you need him,' Mrs Fontana repeated softly.

Lauren looked at Twilight with delight. 'Then everything's OK.' She put her arms round his neck and hugged him close. 'You won't ever have to go away,

Twilight.' She turned to Mrs Fontana.
'We'll be together forever!'

A look full of wisdom and sadness
seemed to cross the old lady's face.
'Maybe,' she murmured.

Walter woofed and glanced down the

path. Mrs Fontana smiled and pulled her
yellow shawl around her shoulders. 'I
must go. Goodnight.'

'Goodnight,' Lauren replied.

Mrs Fontana started to walk away, then
paused and looked back. 'The time you
have together is precious,' she said softly,
her bright eyes flickering intently from
Lauren to Twilight. 'Make the most of it,
my dears.'

Nine

'Lauren! Wait for me!'

Lauren turned on her way in through the school gates the next morning and saw Mel running towards her.

'Hi there,' Lauren said, waiting for her.

'Hi!' Mel said. She looked around. 'Where's Max? Isn't he coming to school today?'

'He's over there,' Lauren said. Max had run on ahead and was already playing ball with his friends. He was laughing and shouting happily.

'Do you want to go for a ride this afternoon?' Mel asked as she and Lauren continued into school.

'Yeah,' Lauren said.

Just then, Nick, Andrew and Dan came cycling past them. Lauren looked at them closely. Their faces were pale.

'Uh-oh,' Mel said, seeing them. 'Max and his friends had better watch out.'

Lauren watched the boys get off their bikes. 'If we go for a ride, we could go down to the creek again,' she said to Mel. She raised her voice so that the boys could hear. 'I want to explore that tree house.'

She saw Mel look at her with astonishment, but her attention was focused on the three boys. At the mention of the words *tree house* they swung round and stared at her.

'The tree house by the creek!' Dan said, looking scared. 'Don't go there – it's haunted!'

'By a headless horseman,' Andrew put in, coming over. 'He was there last night.'

'We saw him,' Dan told them. 'It was horrible!'

Mel's eyes widened with alarm. 'Really?'

'Yeah,' Nick said earnestly. 'I am never

going near that tree house again.' He
looked at Lauren. 'I wouldn't go there if I
were you.'

'I see,' Lauren said innocently.

The boys started to walk off.

'By the way, Nick,' Lauren called. She
rummaged in her bag. 'Is this yours?' As
she spoke, she held out Nick's book.

Nick came over. Taking it, he checked
the inside cover and then stared at her.
'Yes. How did *you* get it?'

Lauren spoke coolly. 'Oh, I found it
when I went to the tree house last night.'

She had to bite back a grin as all three
boys and Mel stared at her as if she'd just
gone crazy.

'*You* went to the tree house last night?'

Nick exclaimed.

'You couldn't have — we were there until it was dark,' Andrew said.

'I went *after* it was dark,' Lauren said.

'Did you see the headless horseman?' Dan demanded.

'I didn't,' Lauren said. She smiled cheerfully. 'But I promise I'll let you guys know if I see him *next* time I'm there.'

She took Mel's arm and smiled sweetly at them. 'See you then,' she said to the boys and, enjoying the speechless looks on their faces, she pulled Mel away.

Rounding a corner out of sight of the boys, Lauren burst out laughing.

Mel stared at her in astonishment. 'OK,' she said, breaking away and putting her hands on her hips. 'What *is* going on?'

Lauren grinned. 'It's a long story. Let's find Jessica and I'll tell you all about it.'

'I am *so* glad this place isn't haunted,' Jessica said as she, Lauren and Mel made themselves at home in the tree house after school. Below them, Shadow and

Twilight were grazing by the creek. 'Now everyone can share it and have fun.'

'Yeah,' Mel agreed, looking around as if she could hardly believe it. 'It'll be great!' She shook her head. 'So, tell us again,' she said to Lauren. 'You rode here and scared Nick and the others by galloping around on Twilight and pretending to be a ghost?'

For about the fiftieth time, Lauren nodded and told the story. 'I heard the boys here after school talking about scaring people and I saw them do it. I knew it wasn't haunted then, so I came back later with Twilight.' She crossed her fingers as she stretched the truth slightly.

'I wore a sheet
and pretended to be a ghost. Because
it was dark, Nick and the others
couldn't see Twilight properly through
the trees and they thought I was a real
ghost – a headless horseman.'

'That's incredible!' Jessica said.

'It was really brave of you to come here on your own at night,' Mel said admiringly to Lauren, 'even if you knew this place wasn't haunted.'

Lauren looked out of the window at Twilight grazing below. 'But I wasn't on my own,' she said, smiling. 'I had Twilight.'

My Secret Unicorn

Stronger Than Magic

As she reached the
paddock, she saw Twilight still
lying where she had left him. His nose
was resting heavily on the ground, his eyes
were closed. 'Twilight!' Lauren cried out.
Twilight's ears flickered and he half-raised his
head. He looked exhausted. Lauren scrambled
over the gate and raced across the grass. Throwing
herself down on the ground beside him, she
touched his neck. 'Twilight!' she
gasped. 'What's the matter? You look
really ill!'

My Secret Unicorn

Stronger Than Magic

Linda Chapman

Illustrated by Biz Hull

PUFFIN

PUFFIN BOOKS

Published by the Penguin Group
Penguin Books Ltd, 80 Strand, London WC2R 0RL, England
Penguin Putnam Inc., 375 Hudson Street, New York, New York 10014, USA
Penguin Books Australia Ltd, 250 Camberwell Road, Camberwell, Victoria 3124, Australia
Penguin Books Canada Ltd, 10 Alcorn Avenue, Toronto, Ontario, Canada M4V 3B2
Penguin Books India (P) Ltd, 11 Community Centre, Panchsheel Park,
New Delhi – 110 017, India
Penguin Books (NZ) Ltd, Cnr Rosedale and Airborne Roads, Albany,
Auckland, New Zealand
Penguin Books (South Africa) (Pty) Ltd, 24 Sturdee Avenue,
Rosebank 2196, South Africa

Penguin Books Ltd, Registered Offices: 80 Strand, London WC2R 0RL, England

www.penguin.com

First published 2003
Published in this edition 2004

1

Text copyright © Working Partners Ltd, 2003
Illustrations copyright © Biz Hull, 2003
Created by Working Partners Ltd, London W6 0QT
All rights reserved

The moral right of the author and illustrator has been asserted

Set in 14.25/21.5pt Bembo

Made and printed in England by Clays Ltd, St Ives plc

British Library Cataloguing in Publication Data
A CIP catalogue record for this book is available from the British Library

ISBN 0-141-31928-3

For Bramble — my own Buddy
— you loved life so much.
I miss you every single day.

One

'I love this place,' Lauren Foster whispered as she sat on Twilight's warm back. Fireflies danced around them, lighting up the dusky shadows of the peaceful forest glade.

Moonlight shone on Twilight's silvery horn as he nodded. 'Me too.'

Lauren patted him. She could hardly believe how lucky she was. Most of the

time, Twilight looked like any ordinary
grey pony, but when she said the words
of the Turning Spell, he transformed
into a magical unicorn and they flew to
places like this secret glade in the
woods.

'When we're here, I feel like anything
could happen,' Lauren said, looking round
at the unusual pinky-grey rocks.

'That's because it's a special place,'
Twilight told her. 'There's magic in the
air.' He snorted softly. 'Shall we stay here
or shall we fly some more?'

Lauren glanced at her watch. 'We
should really go home.'

Lauren's parents had no idea that
Twilight was a unicorn. At the moment,

they just thought she was outside in his paddock, feeding him.

'I could use my unicorn powers to see whether they're worrying,' Twilight suggested. 'If they aren't, we could stay out a little longer.'

'That's a great idea,' Lauren replied.

Twilight trotted over to one of the unusual rocks at the side of the clearing. As a unicorn, he had many magical powers. One of them allowed him to use the rocks of rose quartz to see what was happening anywhere else in the world. Touching his horn to the surface of one, he said, 'Granger's Farm!'

There was a bright purple flash and mist started to swirl. As it cleared, an image of Lauren's home – Granger's Farm – appeared in the rock. Lauren slid off Twilight's back to look more closely. She could see Twilight's paddock, the surrounding fields filled with cows, her bedroom window, her mum's car . . .

'Lauren's mum and dad,' Twilight said to the rock.

The picture wobbled and suddenly Mr and Mrs Foster appeared. They were talking, but all Lauren could hear was a faint buzz. Tucking her long, fair hair behind her ears, she leaned closer to the rock. The buzz turned into voices.

'Is Lauren still outside with Twilight?' she heard her dad say.

Lauren tensed, but to her relief her mum spoke calmly.

'She is, but don't worry. She knows to be in by bedtime. She just likes spending as much time with him as possible,' Mrs Foster said, smiling. 'It's one of the best things about having moved to the

country. Lauren and Max can have so much more freedom. If we were still in the city . . .'

Lauren saw her dad take her mum's hand. 'Moving here was the best thing we ever did,' he said.

Lauren sat back on her heels. 'It's OK,' she said to Twilight. 'I think we're safe for a while.'

'Shall we do some flying then?' Twilight said eagerly.

'In a minute,' Lauren said. She was enjoying looking at her family. 'Can I have a look at Max first?'

'All right,' Twilight said obligingly. 'Max!' he said.

The picture focused to show Max,

Lauren's six-year-old brother. He was
playing in his bedroom with his Bernese
mountain dog puppy, Buddy.

Lauren could tell from the way he was
holding a dog treat in his hand that he
was trying to get Buddy to sit.

She grinned at Twilight. 'Max and Buddy are starting dog-training classes tomorrow.' She watched the picture for a few more seconds. It was fun not being seen. 'Let's have a look at Mel now,' she said to Twilight. 'Just quickly.'

Mel Cassidy was Lauren's neighbour and one of her best friends. Twilight murmured Mel's name and the picture changed to show Mel sitting in her bedroom with her mum. Mrs Cassidy had her arm round Mel's shoulders.

'Mel's crying!' Lauren said in alarm. She started to lean forward and then stopped. Listening to her own family was one thing, but somehow listening in on a friend talking to her mum didn't

seem right. 'I don't know if we should listen,' she said doubtfully.

'But perhaps if we know what's wrong, we can help,' Twilight pointed out.

Lauren hesitated for a moment. She and Twilight were good at helping people in trouble. That's why unicorns came to live in the human world – to use their magical powers to do good deeds with their human owners. She looked at the picture in the rock. Mel looked really upset. Quickly, Lauren made up her mind. 'OK, but we'll only listen for a second,' she said.

Lauren and Twilight leaned closer.

'It's not fair,' she heard Mel say. 'I just can't do it, Mum. I've asked Mr Noland to

explain twice now and I still don't get it!'

'You'll just have to ask Mr Noland to go through it again,' Mrs Cassidy said gently.

Lauren frowned in surprise. Mr Noland was their class teacher. What could be upsetting Mel?

'But then Lauren and Jessica will think I'm really dumb!' Mel cried.

'I'm sure they won't,' Mrs Cassidy said, hugging her. 'They're your friends.'

'But they can do fractions. It's just me who can't!' Mel said.

Fractions! Lauren sat back and the voices faded to a buzz again.

'Fractions?' Twilight said, sounding puzzled. 'What are they?'

'They're something we're doing in maths,' Lauren answered.

'So it's nothing serious then,' Twilight said in relief.

'Well, I don't know.' Lauren hesitated. 'If Mel's upset by it, then it is serious. She seems to think Jessica and I will laugh at her.' She shook her head. 'But we'd never do that. We don't care if she can do fractions or not. She's our friend.' She chewed a fingernail. 'Poor Mel,' she said softly. 'I wish I could help her.'

Twilight looked doubtful. 'I don't think any of my magic powers can help people do maths.'

'I guess not,' Lauren said. 'It looks like

this is one problem I'll have to solve on my own.'

Twilight touched his horn to the rock. With a purple flash the picture disappeared. 'Let's go flying now,' he said.

Lauren didn't need any more encouragement. She vaulted on to Twilight's warm back. Taking two strides, he leapt upwards into the sky.

The wind whipped against Lauren's face and her hair blew out behind her as they swooped through the air before finally flying back to Granger's Farm.

'So, how are you going to help Mel?' Twilight asked her as they landed.

'I'm not sure yet,' Lauren replied. 'But I'll try to think of something by

tomorrow.' She hugged him and said the Undoing Spell.

There was a purple flash and suddenly Twilight was no longer a unicorn but a small grey pony.

'Good night, Twilight,' Lauren whispered.

Twilight whickered softly and, giving him one last hug, Lauren hurried into the house.

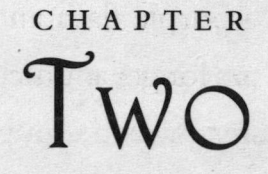

CHAPTER

Two

'Lauren! You're going to be late for school!' Mrs Foster called up the stairs the next morning.

Lauren pulled a brush through her hair and hurried downstairs. School mornings were always a rush. As she ran into the kitchen, she almost fell over Buddy.

'Sit, Buddy! Buddy, sit!' Max was saying.

Seeing Lauren, Buddy leapt up in delight. Lauren tickled his ears. 'Hey, boy,' she said.

'Buddy! Come here and sit!' Max commanded sternly as the puppy gambolled around Lauren's legs.

Buddy crouched down with his front legs and stuck his bottom playfully in the air. 'Woof!' he barked, before bounding off wildly around the kitchen.

'He's going to be just great at obedience classes, Max,' Lauren teased as Buddy skidded to a halt too late and cannoned into the fridge door. 'He'll be bottom of the class.'

'He won't!' Max cried. 'Mum!' He turned to their mum. 'He won't, will he?'

'Buddy will be just fine, honey,' Mrs Foster said reassuringly. 'Lauren, stop teasing Max and eat some breakfast.'

Lauren sat down and buttered a piece of toast. Max was trying to open a new jar of chocolate spread.

'Come on, Max,' Lauren said impatiently. 'We'll be late.'

Max twisted with all his strength but the lid wouldn't come off.

'Here, let me,' Lauren said, taking it from him and opening it in one go.

'Lauren!' Max protested. 'I wanted to do it! You always interfere!'

'We'd have been here all morning,' Lauren told him.

'That's enough, both of you!' Mrs Foster said, running a hand through her hair. 'Finish your toast and let's go.'

'Hi, Lauren!' Jessica Parker called as Lauren ran into the classroom just before the bell rang.

'Hi,' Lauren said. She still hadn't thought of a plan to help Mel and it was troubling her.

'Samantha and I were looking at ponies for sale in a magazine last night,' Jessica told Lauren. 'There were three that we liked the sound of. We've been trying to get Dad to ring up about them.'

'Any luck?' Lauren asked. She knew how desperate Jessica and her stepsister were to have a pony.

Jessica sighed. 'No. Dad says we've got to wait until the summer holidays.'

Just then, Mel hurried into the classroom.

'Hi,' Lauren said.

'Hello,' Mel replied. Lauren noticed

that her voice was much quieter than usual.

Before they could say anything else, the bell rang and Mr Noland came into the classroom. 'Quiet, please!' he said, clapping his hands.

As Mr Noland took the register, Lauren watched Mel. She was looking pale and unhappy.

'OK, everyone, maths books out, please,' Mr Noland said as he put the register away. 'I'd like you to work through exercise three on page twenty-two.'

They fetched their maths books and quiet fell as everyone began working. Lauren could see that Mel was staring at

the page of fractions, a panicky look on her face.

'Are you stuck?' Lauren whispered to her. 'I can help if you like.'

'No . . . no, I'm just thinking,' Mel replied as she hastily scribbled down an answer.

Lauren wracked her brains. She wanted to help Mel, but how?

'You don't seem to have done very much, Lauren.' Mr Noland's voice behind her made Lauren jump. 'Do you need some help?'

Lauren looked up guiltily. 'No, I'm fine . . .' she started to say but then she stopped. She'd had an idea. 'Actually, I do need help, please,' she said quickly. 'I'm confused.'

Mr Noland looked surprised. 'But you've been managing fractions OK all week. What seems to be the problem?' He leaned over her desk. 'All you have to do is put the fractions in order, smallest first. You need to consider both the

denominator and the numerator –'

'The numerator is the number on top of the fraction and the denominator is the number on the bottom of the fraction, isn't it?' Lauren said, stopping him before he could race on ahead like he usually did.

'Yes and –'

'A fraction is just a small part of a whole, isn't it, Mr Noland?' Lauren said quickly. 'Like one piece of a whole cake. The denominator – the bottom number – tells you how many pieces the cake has been cut into and the numerator – the top number – tells you how many pieces of cake you have.' She glanced quickly to the side and was relieved to

see that Mel was listening.

'Yes, that's right,' said Mr Noland, starting to sound a bit impatient.

'So, if the fraction is one third – one over three – the denominator is three which means the cake has been cut into three pieces,' she went on.

'Yes,' Mr Noland replied. 'And if you see the fraction one fifth – one over five – the denominator is . . .?'

Before Lauren could answer, Mel spoke up. 'Five?'

Lauren and Mr Noland looked round.

'That's right, Mel,' Mr Noland said.

'Which means the cake has been cut into five pieces. And the fraction one tenth would mean the cake had been cut

into ten pieces,' Mel said, her eyes starting to light up. 'One fifth is bigger than one tenth because if you cut a cake into five pieces, each slice of the cake is bigger than if you'd cut it into ten pieces.'

'That's right,' Mr Noland said to her.

Mel's eyes were shining. 'It suddenly all makes sense.'

'Well, that's great,' Mr Noland said. 'How about you, Lauren? Do you understand now?'

'Me?' Lauren caught herself. 'Oh, yes. Thank you, Mr Noland.'

Mr Noland smiled. 'Well, I'm glad you're happier.'

Lauren looked at the relief on Mel's face and smiled. 'Yes,' she said, feeling warm inside. 'I'm much happier now!'

Lauren was still glowing when she got home after school. 'You should have seen Mel's face when she finally worked out

fractions,' she told Twilight as she
groomed him before tacking him up to
take him out on a ride with Mel and her
pony, Shadow. 'She looked so relieved.'

Twilight snorted. When he was a pony
he couldn't talk to her, but Lauren knew
he understood every word she said.

'It kind of made me think,' Lauren said
as she cleaned out the curry-comb. 'I
know we try and help people when
they've got big problems – like helping
Jessica when she was really upset about
her dad getting remarried, but couldn't
we also use your powers to help those
with smaller problems too? Sometimes
people get almost as upset over
something little as over something big.'

She looked at Twilight. He looked as though he was listening hard. 'What do you think?'

Twilight nodded his head.

Lauren hugged him. 'It'll be evening soon,' she whispered. 'We can talk properly then.'

CHAPTER

Three

Lauren was untacking Twilight after her ride with Mel when Buddy and Max came charging down the path that led from the house to the paddock.

'We've been at obedience class,' Max burst out. 'Buddy was brilliant! The teacher said he was the best puppy there!'

'That's great,' Lauren said, smiling.

'He learned to sit and lie down and

stay,' said Max. 'Watch!' Taking a handful of dog treats out of his pocket, Max called Buddy. 'Buddy! Here, boy!'

Buddy trotted over. 'Sit!' Max said firmly, holding the treat above Buddy's head.

To Lauren's amazement, Buddy sat.

'And lie down,' Max said, lowering the treat.

Buddy did as he was told. 'Now stay,' Max said. He walked once round Buddy and then gave him the treat. 'Good boy!' he cried. 'You did it!'

'Wow,' Lauren said, impressed.

'I can't wait until tomorrow's class,' Max said happily. 'We're going to learn how to get the puppies to walk on a

lead. Here, boy,' he called to Buddy, who was snuffling happily in Twilight's grooming kit. 'Let's practise.'

'Maybe it would be best to give Buddy a rest,' Lauren suggested. 'Before he gets tired of learning. We could play hide and seek.'

It was a game that she and Max had just taught Buddy. One of them held the puppy while the other went and hid and then Buddy found them.

'OK,' Max said.

Lauren turned Twilight out in the paddock and then she and Max took it in turns to hide. Buddy found them every time. It was great fun and even Twilight stopped grazing to look.

'Twilight's watching us!' Max
exclaimed, as he tried to push Buddy off
his tummy. 'Buddy! Get off!' he cried as
Buddy licked his nose.

Twilight whinnied. Lauren smiled. It
sounded almost as though he were
laughing.

*

'I'm just going out to see Twilight, Mum,' Lauren said, pulling her trainers on after supper.

'OK, honey,' Mrs Foster replied. She stood up and looked over to where Max was playing with Buddy. 'Come on, Max, time for your bath.'

Lauren ran down to the paddock. She couldn't wait to find out what Twilight thought of her plan about helping people with little problems as well as big.

'So, what do you think?' she asked as soon as he was a unicorn again.

'It's a good idea,' Twilight answered. 'The more people we can help, the better.'

Lauren grinned in delight. 'I was hoping you'd say that!'

'There are some rocks of rose quartz over there,' Twilight said, nodding in the direction of a cluster of trees at the end of his paddock. 'We could check who needs help right now.'

'OK!' Lauren mounted and they cantered down the paddock. Not for the first time, Lauren felt thankful that Twilight's paddock was well hidden from the house. She and Twilight should be safe in the shadow of the trees.

'There they are,' Twilight said, pointing his horn at several small boulders under an oak tree.

'Let's see Mel first,' Lauren said eagerly.

Within a few seconds, a picture had appeared in the rock, showing Mel snuggled up to her mum on the sofa.

'She looks much happier,' Twilight said, pleased.

Lauren nodded. 'OK, let's try Jessica.'

Twilight said Jessica's name and the picture changed. Jessica was sitting in the kitchen talking to her dad. She was frowning. Lauren leaned forward to find out why Jessica was looking so miserable.

'But I really wanted a pony, Dad,' Jessica was saying.

'It'll be easier to find one in the summer holidays,' Mr Parker replied. 'We'll have more time.'

Lauren sighed. She knew Jessica

wanted a pony right now, but she didn't
see how she and Twilight could help with
that. She was about to ask him to look at
someone else when Jessica said something
that caught her attention.

'But I get left out, Dad,' she said.
'Lauren and Mel meet after school to go
riding together and I can't join in. Like
this afternoon, they went riding together
and I couldn't go with them.'

Lauren sat back. 'Did you hear that?'

Twilight nodded. 'It can't be much fun
for Jessica seeing you and Mel riding
together.' He shook his mane. 'But it's
easy to solve. When you and Mel next
meet up, ask Jessica to join you. You can
take it in turns to ride me and Shadow.'

'Good idea,' Lauren said. Fired up by
thinking how easy it would be to solve
Jessica's unhappiness, she looked at the
rock again. 'OK, let's see if anyone else in
my class is unhappy.' She started
suggesting different names. A little
niggling feeling ran through her. She
knew she shouldn't really be listening in
on other people's conversations. Still, it
was for the best, wasn't it? It was so she
could help them.

Lauren got so engrossed in seeing the
other kids from her class going about
their everyday lives – watching TV,
reading, doing homework – that she
almost forgot that she was supposed to be
looking for someone who was unhappy.

She was relieved – everyone seemed to
be doing just fine. She glanced at her
watch. 'I hadn't realized it was so late.'
She stood up. 'We've only got ten
minutes before I have to go in. We'll just
have time to have a very quick fly-round
tonight.'

'Let's go then,' Twilight said, touching his horn to the rock and making the picture disappear. Lauren mounted and held on to his mane.

Twilight started to trot forward, but then suddenly stopped. 'I feel tired,' he said, sounding surprised.

'Tired?' Lauren echoed.

'Yes, sort of achy but . . . but . . .' Twilight looked confused. 'It's strange — I never normally feel tired when I'm a unicorn.'

'We don't have to fly tonight,' Lauren said, concerned. 'Maybe you're not well.'

'No, I'll be fine,' Twilight replied bravely. 'Let's try again.' He trotted forward and this time took off into the

sky. Lauren felt the cool wind streaming against her face. She leaned forward. They were flying again!

But soon she started to feel worried. Twilight seemed to be going slower than usual. Normally he galloped and swooped lightly and easily, but tonight his movements felt heavy and slow.

'Are you OK?' she asked.

'I . . . I feel a little strange,' Twilight replied.

'Let's go down,' Lauren said quickly.

Twilight didn't argue. Turning, he flew back to the paddock.

As he landed, Lauren slid off his back. He was breathing heavily. 'What's wrong?' she asked.

'I don't know,' he answered.

'Maybe you're coming down with some sort of bug,' Lauren said anxiously. 'Shall I get Dad to call the vet?'

Twilight shook his head. 'I don't feel ill. Just tired. I'll probably be better in the morning.'

'I'll turn you back into a pony and make you a warm bran mash,' Lauren said. 'That might help.'

Twilight nodded and Lauren said the Undoing Spell. Then, going to the feed room, she put several scoops of bran, a handful of oats and some salt into a

bucket and added hot water. Mixing it all up, she carried it back to Twilight. 'Here, boy, eat this.'

Twilight whickered gratefully and plunged his nose into the bucket.

As he ate, Lauren kissed his head. *Oh, Twilight,* she thought, biting her lip, *please be OK.*

CHAPTER

Four

L auren didn't sleep well that night. As soon as she woke up, she looked out of her window. Twilight was standing by the gate. Pulling on her clothes, Lauren hurried outside.

'Are you feeling better now?' she asked.

To her relief, Twilight nodded.

Lauren rubbed his forehead. 'I've been so worried,' she told him softly.

'I don't think I could bear you to be ill.'

'Do you want to go for a ride this
evening?' Mel asked Lauren as they got
their books out that morning.

'Yes – if Twilight's OK,' Lauren replied.

'What's the matter with him?' Jessica
asked, looking concerned.

'He didn't seem very well last night,'
Lauren said. 'He was tired.'

'Maybe he's got a cold,' Mel suggested.
'Shadow sometimes gets them. They
make him a bit quiet, but they're not
serious. So, do you want to meet up?' she
asked. 'We could ride at mine instead of
going out, then, if Twilight seems tired,
you can always go home.'

'OK,' Lauren replied. She happened to glance at Jessica and caught a look of unhappiness fleeting across her face. 'Hey, Jess,' Lauren said quickly, 'why don't you meet us as well? We can take it in turns to ride.'

'Yeah,' Mel said, looking at Jessica. 'That's a great idea.'

'Really? Are you sure you don't mind?' Jessica said hesitantly.

'Of course not,' Lauren told her and Mel shook her head.

'OK then,' Jessica said, smiling. 'Thanks. I'll see if Dad will drop me off.'

To Lauren's relief, Twilight seemed to be back to his normal self when she got

home from school that afternoon. He whinnied when he saw her coming.

'Do you feel well enough to go round to Mel's?' she asked him.

Twilight nodded. Feeling much happier, Lauren groomed him and saddled up.

Jessica was already at Mel's house when Lauren and Twilight arrived and the three girls had lots of fun timing themselves as they took it in turns to ride Shadow and Twilight around an obstacle course in Shadow's paddock.

'I've had a great time,' Jessica said happily as they let the ponies graze afterwards while they ate home-made cookies.

'We'll have to do this again,' Lauren
said. 'It's more fun when there are three
of us.'

'Yeah, definitely,' Mel said. 'Until you
get your own pony, you can ride Shadow
as much as you like, Jess.'

'And Twilight,' Lauren said.

Jessica's eyes shone happily. 'Thanks, guys. You're the best friends ever!'

'Jessica really enjoyed herself today,' Lauren said to Twilight that night after she had turned him into a unicorn.

'I'm glad we found out that she was upset,' Twilight said.

Lauren nodded. 'Let's have a look and see if there's anyone else who needs our help.'

They went down to the end of the field where the rose-quartz rocks were. The first person Lauren and Twilight saw was a boy in her class, David Andrews, with his father.

'They look like they're arguing,' Lauren

said, leaning closer to the rock.

'I'm not going to wear them!' David was saying.

'Yes, you are,' his dad replied firmly. 'And I've written to Mr Noland asking him to make sure that you do.'

'Dad!' David cried.

'It's for the best,' his dad said. He shook his head. 'David, lots of people wear glasses . . .'

Lauren looked at Twilight. 'Glasses!' she exclaimed. 'That's all that's upsetting David – he's got to wear glasses.'

'Well, if you tell him how good his glasses look, it might help,' Twilight suggested.

'It's worth a try,' Lauren agreed. 'Come

on, let's look at some other people.'

Most of the other kids seemed happy enough, apart from Joanne Bailey. Joanne sat at the table next to Lauren and she was miserable because her computer had broken down. She couldn't do the geography research that Mr Noland had asked them to do by the next day.

'I can easily help with that,' Lauren said. 'I'll print out some extra research from the Internet and take it in tomorrow for Joanne to use –'

'Lauren,' Twilight interrupted. 'I . . . I feel strange again.'

Lauren looked at him in concern. 'It's my fault. I shouldn't have made you do that obstacle course at Mel's.'

'But I was feeling all right then,'
Twilight said. 'It's just now – I feel tired
all of a sudden.' He shook his head
wearily. 'Can we stop doing the magic
now? I think I'd better change back.'

'Of course,' Lauren said, jumping to
her feet.

Once Twilight was a pony again, he lay down. Lauren watched him, feeling very worried. What was the matter with him? He was never tired or ill. And this was twice now in two days.

'I'll leave my window open tonight,' she whispered. 'Whinny if you want anything and I'll come straight down.'

Twilight snorted softly and closed his eyes.

Lauren kept her window open all night just as she had promised. At six o'clock, she jumped out of bed and crossed the room to look out. But Twilight wasn't by the gate. Lauren felt alarmed. Twilight always stood there in the morning.

Pulling on her jeans, she hurried outside.

As she reached the paddock, she saw Twilight still lying where she had left him. His nose was resting heavily on the ground and his eyes were closed.

'Twilight!' Lauren cried out.

Twilight's ears flickered and he half–raised his head. He looked exhausted.

Lauren scrambled over the gate and raced across the grass. Throwing herself down on the ground beside him, she touched his neck. 'Twilight!' she gasped. 'What's the matter? You look really ill!'

Twilight snorted weakly.

'I'm going to get Dad!' Lauren said, jumping to her feet. 'Don't worry, Twilight. I'll be back as soon as I can.'

CHAPTER

Five

M r Foster was very worried when
he saw Twilight. 'I'm going to call
the vet,' he said.

As he hurried off, Lauren crouched
down beside her pony. 'You're going to
be OK,' she told him, her eyes stinging
with hot tears. 'We'll find out what's
wrong with you, I promise.'

Tony Blackstone, their vet, arrived

within the hour. He took Twilight's
temperature and monitored his heart rate,
then he ran his hands all over Twilight's
body.

'Has Twilight been off-colour for a
while?' he asked Lauren.

'He seemed tired the day before
yesterday,' she replied, 'but otherwise he's
been fine.'

'So he hasn't had a cough, or runny
nose, or been restless and wanting to roll?'

'No,' Lauren replied.

Tony continued his examination, but at
last he shook his head. 'Well, it's puzzling.
If it weren't for the way he's acting, I'd
say he seems to be a very healthy pony.
I'll take a blood test and see what shows up.

Maybe he's got a virus.'

'Is there anything we can do?' Mr
Foster asked.

'Call me if he gets any worse, but
otherwise just let him rest. I'll ring you

with the test results as soon as I have them.' Tony shot Lauren a comforting glance. 'Don't worry. I'm sure he's going to be just fine.'

Lauren thought about Twilight all the way to school. What if there was something seriously wrong with him? A cold feeling clenched at her heart.

Walking into the cloakroom, she saw Joanne Bailey talking to her friend, Rachel. Lauren suddenly remembered about the extra research that she had printed out. 'Hi,' she said to them, as she put her coat on the peg. 'Did you do the geography homework last night?'

'Yeah,' Rachel replied.

'I couldn't,' Joanne said. 'My computer broke down.'

'I've got some extra if you need some more,' Lauren offered eagerly.

'It's OK, thanks,' Joanne replied. 'Rachel's lent me some of hers.'

'Are you sure?' Lauren asked, taking out the papers. 'I have them right here.'

'No, really, I'm fine,' Joanne said, and turned back to continue her conversation with Rachel.

Feeling disappointed that her plan to help hadn't worked out as she'd hoped, Lauren went into the classroom. As she walked through the door, she saw David talking with a group of his friends. She stopped. David had his new glasses on

but, to her relief, his friends didn't seem
to be teasing him.

Just then, David glanced up and caught
her watching him. 'What are you looking
at?' he asked suspiciously.

'Nothing,' Lauren replied.

'It must be your glasses,' one of David's
friends sniggered.

'It isn't!' Lauren said quickly, seeing
David go red. 'They're . . . they're very
nice glasses.'

David's friends burst out laughing.

'Lauren likes you, David!' one of them
said.

'Lauren Foster wants to be your
girlfriend.'

'No, I don't!' Lauren exclaimed.

She hurried to her desk, her own
cheeks burning. As she went, she could
hear David's friends start to tease him
about how girls really liked boys with
glasses. *Oh, great,* Lauren thought in
dismay. *I haven't helped David at all – in*

fact, it looks like I've made things worse!

To her relief, Mel and Jessica arrived and she didn't have to listen to David's friends any more.

After school, Lauren went straight to see Twilight. To her relief, he whinnied when he saw her and trotted over to the gate. Lauren's heart rose. He looked much happier.

She got out her grooming kit and spent ages brushing him and combing out every tangle in his mane and tail. As she worked, she told him about David and Joanne. 'They didn't seem to need my help,' she said. 'In fact, I think I made things worse for David by saying that his

glasses were nice. His friends started teasing him then.' She sighed. 'I wish you could talk back, but I won't turn you into a unicorn tonight. You've got to rest.'

Twilight nuzzled her.

'I'm going to go and get you some carrots,' Lauren said. 'I'll be back in a minute.'

She hurried to the house. Her dad was in the kitchen with Max. They had just got back from dog-training class and Max was putting Buddy's lead away.

Lauren took three carrots from the fridge. Buddy came over to see what she was doing. She patted him. 'How was Buddy's lesson? Is he still top of the class?'

'No,' Max said, stomping over and sitting down. 'No, he isn't.' Buddy tried to put his head on Max's knee, but Max pushed him away.

Mr Foster sighed. 'Buddy wasn't very good today,' he explained to Lauren. 'They were trying to teach the puppies to fetch a toy, but Buddy just kept running off and not coming back.'

Max stared at the floor.

'Don't worry,' Lauren said sympathetically. 'I'm sure Buddy will learn soon.'

'Lauren's right, Max,' Mr Foster said. 'You've got all weekend to teach Buddy how to fetch. There isn't another class until Monday.'

Lauren bent down and stroked the puppy. 'He'll learn to fetch, won't you, Buddy?'

Looking up at her, Buddy wagged his tail.

The next morning, Tony Blackstone came to check on Twilight again. 'Nothing obvious has shown up on the blood test,' he told Lauren and Mr Foster, 'but I'll send it off to the lab for further analysis. Still, I'm sure there's nothing to worry about. He looks better already, don't you, boy?'

Twilight whickered.

Tony smiled. 'You'd almost think he could understand what I was saying.'

Lauren only just managed to hide her grin. *If only he knew!* 'Should he rest today?' she asked.

'Yes, just to be on the safe side,' Tony said.

As Mr Foster walked with the vet back to his car, Max picked up a stick and threw it. 'Go, boy!' he called to Buddy. 'Go fetch!'

Buddy bounded up to the stick and grabbed it.

'That's it! Bring it here, Buddy!' Max called.

Buddy wagged his tail, the stick firmly clenched in his teeth.

'Buddy, come here!' Max said, his voice rising in exasperation. He started to walk

towards the puppy, but Buddy dodged
around Max and gambolled away up the
path.

'Buddy!' Max shouted crossly. 'Come
back!'

But Buddy ignored him and galloped
out of sight.

'You could try keeping him on a lead,'

Lauren suggested as Max stared after him.
'Then he couldn't get away.'

'I *know* how to train him, Lauren,' Max
snapped. 'You don't need to tell me.'

'I was only trying to help,' Lauren told
him.

'Well, I don't need your help!' Max
said. 'I —'

Mrs Foster appeared at the top of the path. 'Max!' she interrupted them. 'Can you go and get your swimming things, please? We don't want to be late.'

Max ran off as Mrs Foster walked down to Lauren. 'Do you want to come into town with us, honey?'

Lauren shook her head. 'I'll stay here with Twilight.'

'OK,' her mum said. 'Dad's around. If you need anything, just ask.'

After her mum and Max had driven away, Lauren groomed Twilight and then set to work cleaning his tack and tidying the tack room. By mid-morning everything was spotless.

Lauren went down to the paddock where Twilight was grazing. She sighed. There wasn't much else she could do. Unless . . .

Lauren looked round. Her dad was out on the farm and there was no one else nearby. If she turned Twilight into a unicorn, they could at least talk. Maybe they could even look to see if there were some more people to help. That wouldn't be too tiring. All he'd have to do was touch his horn to a rock.

She led Twilight to the shadow of the trees and said the magic words.

'So, how are you feeling?' she asked as soon as Twilight was a unicorn again.

'Not too bad,' Twilight answered. 'Just a

bit weak and . . .' He pawed at the ground with his hoof. 'Anyway, I'm feeling better than I did yesterday.'

'I was so frightened,' Lauren said. 'I thought you were terribly ill.' She looked towards the bottom of the field. 'Can we go and use your magic powers? I want to see if there's anyone else I can help.' She sighed. 'I didn't exactly do that well with David and Joanne yesterday.'

'At least you tried,' Twilight said reassuringly.

'I guess,' Lauren said as they went over to one of the rocks.

'When will your mum and Max be back?' Twilight asked.

'Probably not for ages yet,' Lauren

replied. 'But we could check and see where they are just to be on the safe side.'

Twilight nodded and, touching his horn to a rock, he murmured, 'Mrs Foster and Max.'

The picture in the rock showed Mrs Foster and Max having a drink in town. Lauren leaned closer. 'I'm never going to get Buddy to fetch,' Max was saying.

'Oh, Max!' Mrs Foster said. 'You've only been trying for one day. Just be patient.'

'Poor Max,' Lauren said to Twilight. 'He's really unhappy that Buddy won't –' She broke off. 'I've had an idea!' she said, her eyes widening. 'Why don't I teach

Buddy to fetch? Just think how pleased
Max would be to get back and find that
Buddy could do it after all!'

Twilight didn't answer. He was rubbing
his head against his leg as if it hurt.

Lauren looked at him in concern. 'Are
you OK?'

'I'm feeling strange,' Twilight replied
weakly. 'I think I need to rest.'

'I'll turn you back,' Lauren said
immediately.

As soon as Twilight was a pony again
he sighed and half-shut his eyes.

Lauren stroked his face. 'Do you want
anything?'

Twilight shook his head.

'OK,' Lauren said. 'Well, I'll be by the

stable with Buddy. If you need me, just whinny.'

She went to find Buddy. The puppy was asleep in the kitchen. He got up eagerly when Lauren came in.

'Come on, boy,' Lauren said, taking a packet of dog treats, a long dog lead and a toy from the cupboard. 'I'm going to teach you to fetch.'

Taking Buddy outside, she clipped on his lead. 'I'm going to throw this toy,' she told him. 'And I want you to bring it back.'

Buddy woofed in excitement as he looked at the orange plastic duck in her hand.

'Go on then, boy,' Lauren said,

throwing the
toy. 'Go fetch!'

Buddy raced after the
duck, grabbed it and then, just as he had
done with Max, he started to bound
away. But this time, the lead pulled him
up short. He stopped in surprise and
shook his head.

Lauren held out a dog treat. 'Here, boy,'
she encouraged.

Buddy looked at her and tried to back
off but the lead held him tight.

Lauren waved the dog treat. 'Come on,
Buddy.'

Buddy hesitated for a moment and
then seemed to make up his mind. Still
holding the toy, he trotted over to her.

'Good boy!' Lauren cried as he
dropped the plastic duck and eagerly
gobbled up the treat. She made a fuss of
him and then stood up. 'OK. Let's try that
again.'

Twenty minutes later, Buddy had got the
hang of fetching the toy. As soon as he
picked it up, he carried it back to Lauren,
knowing that a treat was waiting for him.

'You are *such* a clever boy,' Lauren praised him after he had done it without the lead attached. 'Max is going to be so pleased!'

Buddy wagged his tail and, leaving him to play, Lauren went back to check on Twilight.

He was lying down in the paddock. Lauren knelt down beside him. 'Twilight? How are you feeling? Shall I get Dad to call the vet?'

Twilight shook his head and rested his muzzle on her knees.

'Oh, Twilight,' Lauren said. 'I wish I knew what the matter was.' She massaged his ears and he sighed.

✶

Lauren wasn't sure how long she'd been sitting with Twilight when the silence was broken by the sound of Max's voice.

'Buddy! Where are you?' Max came running down the path to the paddock. Buddy woofed in delight and bounded over to say hello.

Seeing Twilight lying down, Max stopped in concern. 'Is Twilight sick again, Lauren?'

Lauren stood up. Her legs felt stiff from sitting on the ground for so long. 'He just seems tired.'

'Poor Twilight,' Max said. 'I hope he gets better soon.' He patted Buddy. 'Come on, Buddy. Now that I'm back I'm going to teach you to fetch.'

Lauren remembered her good news. 'You don't have to,' she said, smiling.

'What do you mean?' Max said in surprise.

'I taught him while you were out. Watch this.' Seeing the toy duck lying by the gate, Lauren picked it up and threw it. 'Fetch, Buddy!'

Buddy trotted over, picked the duck up and brought it back. 'Good boy!' Lauren exclaimed, feeding him a dog treat from her pocket.

She turned to Max, her eyes shining. 'What do you think?'

To her surprise, she saw Max was frowning crossly at her. 'But Buddy's my dog. I wanted to teach him!' he cried.

'I was just trying to help,'
Lauren said.

'No, you weren't.' Max
looked close to tears. 'You just
wanted to show that you
could do it and I
couldn't!'

'Max —' Lauren began.

But Max wouldn't listen. 'You always interfere, Lauren! You always ruin things!' Pushing past her, he ran off into the woods at the side of the paddock.

Lauren watched him go, feeling awful. She wanted Max to be pleased. She hadn't meant to upset him. But now that she thought about it, she could see what he meant. Perhaps training Buddy hadn't been a good idea. How would she feel if someone had done the same thing with Twilight? She wondered whether to go after him, but decided it was best to leave him until he'd calmed down.

With a sigh, she turned and went to find her mum to tell her about Twilight.

★

'I'll call Tony,' Mrs Foster said, looking at Twilight lying down in his field. 'Have you been riding this morning?'

'No, we just –' Lauren broke off. 'Well, we just stayed in the field.'

'So there's no reason why he should be tired,' Mrs Foster said.

Lauren shook her head. All Twilight had done that morning was some magic. A thought struck her and she almost gasped out loud. *Magic!* Of course! Why hadn't she thought about it before?

CHAPTER

Six

Lauren's thoughts raced. Every time Twilight had started feeling strange, he had been in his unicorn form doing magic. Maybe he had some sort of special unicorn illness. That would explain why Tony Blackstone couldn't find anything wrong with him!

As her mum went back to the house to ring the vet, Lauren ran to Twilight.

'Twilight!' she said urgently.

Twilight looked up.

'I've had an idea. Maybe it's not the pony bit of you that's sick,' she said, 'maybe it's the *unicorn* bit! You always seem to be ill just after we've done some magic.'

Twilight looked thoughtful but Lauren couldn't tell exactly what he was thinking. She was filled with frustration. If only she could turn him into a unicorn and ask him what he thought, but she couldn't. Not in the middle of his field in broad daylight with her mum around. Then she had an idea.

'Maybe my book on unicorns will have something on unicorn illnesses,' she

said. 'After all, that's where I found the words for the Turning Spell.'

Twilight bowed his head, as if in agreement.

'I'll be back later,' she said, almost running into her mum coming in the opposite direction.

'What's the matter?' her mum said in alarm. 'Has Twilight got worse?'

'No,' Lauren said. 'There's no change in him.'

'Well, I spoke to Tony,' her mum said. 'He's out on call at the moment and can't come over, but he said he'll ring in a few hours and see if there's any improvement.'

Lauren nodded. 'Thanks, Mum.' And before her mum could ask her what she

was doing she raced on to the house and up to her bedroom. There she picked up the battered blue book lying by her bed and sat down. Turning to the front page, she scanned down the five chapter headings.

Chapter One:
Noah and the Unicorns
Chapter Two:
Arcadia
Chapter Three:
Unicorn Myths
Chapter Four:
Unicorn Habits
Chapter Five:
Unicorns and Humans

Lauren frowned. None of them seemed
to be about illnesses. She looked at the
list again. She knew the first chapter
about Noah and the unicorns almost by
heart now, but maybe one of the others
might have something useful in them.
Opening the book at the second chapter,
she started to read.

Half an hour later, a knock at the door
made her look up. 'Lauren?' her mum
said, looking round the door. 'Have you
seen Max?'

'No.' Lauren's head was swirling with
unicorn facts. 'No, I haven't.'

'He must be outside somewhere with
Buddy,' Mrs Foster said. 'I'll call him. It'll

be lunchtime in five minutes.'

Lauren nodded. She just had a few more pages to read.

Mrs Foster left and Lauren turned back to the last chapter. She hadn't found out anything about unicorn illnesses and she was starting to feel increasingly desperate. The last chapter was all about what unicorns did on Earth. Lauren skimmed over the words. She knew most of it already. She read the last paragraph.

Magic is a very powerful force. It must be used wisely or it will exact a powerful toll. Only when a unicorn's powers are used to help those who are truly in need, will the unicorn be strengthened and his powers replenished.

Lauren frowned at the words. What did they mean? She thought she understood the last sentence – if Twilight did good, then he would become stronger. Well, that was all right. They'd been doing loads of good recently. He should be extra strong.

'Lauren!' her mum called from downstairs. 'Can you come here, please?'

Lauren sighed and shut the book. She'd found out absolutely nothing about unicorns getting ill. Maybe they *didn't* get sick. Maybe her idea had been wrong after all.

She walked slowly downstairs. As she went into the kitchen, she stopped in surprise. She'd been expecting to see Max

and her mum sitting at the table ready to eat lunch. But there was no sign of Max, and her mum was standing by the sink, looking worried.

'I can't find Max anywhere,' Mrs Foster said. 'I've been calling him, but he hasn't come in.'

Lauren frowned. 'Maybe he's playing with Buddy.'

'Buddy's here,' her mum said, pointing under the table.

Lauren's stomach tightened. Max hardly ever went off without his puppy.

'When did you last see him?' Mrs Foster asked her.

'It was just after you got back from swimming,' Lauren replied. Just then, she

remembered the argument and her cheeks flushed. 'We had a bit of a fight.'

'What sort of a fight?' her mum asked quickly.

'I'd taught Buddy to fetch while you were out,' Lauren said. 'I was just trying to help but Max got really cross and ran off into the woods. I didn't mean to upset him, Mum.'

'Oh, Lauren,' Mrs Foster sighed. 'I understand, but I can see why Max got angry. It's hard for him being the youngest. Sometimes it must seem to him as if you do everything before him. Training Buddy is the first thing he's ever done on his own.'

'I know, I should have realized,' Lauren said regretfully.

'I'd better call your dad on his mobile phone,' Mrs Foster said. 'Perhaps Max is with him.'

Lauren watched anxiously as her mum made the call. She could tell from her face that it wasn't good news.

Mrs Foster replaced the receiver. 'Your dad hasn't seen Max. He's coming back to help us look.' She twisted her hands together. 'Which way did Max go when he ran off, Lauren?'

'Into the woods,' Lauren replied.

'That must have been about an hour and a half ago,' Mrs Foster said, checking her watch. 'I'll try ringing his friends. Maybe he went to one of their houses. Otherwise we'd better start searching.'

None of Max's friends had seen him, and when Mr Foster got back he and two of the farmhands, Tom and Hank, set out to look in the woods.

'Max could be anywhere,' Mrs Foster

said to Lauren. 'He could still be walking or he might be hiding or . . .' her voice faltered, 'he might be hurt.'

'It'll be OK, Mum,' Lauren said quickly. An idea had come to her.

Mrs Foster nodded and took a deep breath. 'Yes, you're right,' she said, as if she were trying to convince herself. 'It will.' She shook her head. 'Oh, if only we knew which direction he'd gone. I just want him home.'

'I . . . I'm just going to see Twilight,' Lauren said.

Mrs Foster nodded distractedly. 'I'll stay by the phone.'

Lauren ran down to Twilight's field. Twilight had stood up and was by the gate.

'Twilight!' Lauren burst out. 'I know you're not well, but Max has run away and no one knows where he is – I really need your help. Please can I turn you into a unicorn? It would just be for a few minutes so that you can use your magic to see if we can find out where Max is. I wouldn't ask but . . .'

Twilight was already nodding his head up and down.

'Oh, thank you!' Lauren gasped.

Twilight started to trot to the trees. Lauren ran after him. As soon as they reached the safety of the shadows, Lauren said the magic words.

As she spoke the last line of the verse, she tensed expectantly.

There was a pause. For one awful
moment, Lauren thought that the spell
wasn't going to work, but then there was
a weak purple flash and Twilight was
suddenly a unicorn again.

'What happened then?' Lauren gasped.

'I don't know. It felt very strange,' Twilight replied, looking confused.

'I thought you weren't going to change,' Lauren said, her heart pounding.

'Let's not worry about it now,' Twilight said quickly. 'We need to find out where Max is.' He touched his horn to the nearest rose-quartz rock. 'I want to see Max!'

Lauren and Twilight waited. They looked at each other.

Nothing had happened!

CHAPTER
Seven

'It hasn't worked,' Lauren said, looking round. 'Maybe it's the wrong sort of rock. Try that one.' She pointed desperately to another.

Twilight trotted over. 'Max!' he said, touching his horn to the hard surface.

Again, nothing. Lauren looked horrified.

'Your magic's not working!' she
exclaimed.

Twilight looked totally bewildered. 'I
don't feel right. I feel drained, as if,' he
looked at her in alarm, 'as if all my
magic's been used up.'

His words sent a shock through
Lauren. 'Used up? But it can't be!'

'That's how it feels,' Twilight said.

'But the unicorn book said that when
unicorns do good they get stronger and
their magic gets replenished,' Lauren said.
'We've been doing lots of good deeds.
You should have loads of magic.'

'What did it say *exactly*?' Twilight asked
urgently.

Lauren tried to remember. 'It was

something about how a unicorn's magic mustn't be used lightly. I'll go and get it!'

She raced back to the house and returned a few minutes later with the book. 'Here,' she said, and she read out the last paragraph.

Magic is a very powerful force. It must be used wisely or it will exact a powerful toll. Only when a unicorn's powers are used to help those who are truly in need, will the unicorn be strengthened and –

She broke off with a gasp. 'Oh no! That's it!'

'What?' Twilight demanded.

'Don't you see?' Lauren said, pointing to the book. 'We've been trying to help

everyone with all their little everyday problems, not people who are truly in need, so your magic hasn't been strengthened, it's just been used up. A toll is something you pay; well, maybe you're having to pay for how we've been using your magic. Maybe that's why you've been feeling ill!'

Twilight stared at her. 'You might be right.'

Tears sprang to Lauren's eyes. 'What are we going to do? Now we really need your magic to help find Max, we can't use it because there's none left.'

Twilight nuzzled her. 'Don't worry. We can still help to find Max even if we can't use my magic. There must be another way.'

He pawed at the ground, as if trying to think. A stick cracked beneath his hoof. 'I know what to do!' he said suddenly. 'Get Buddy and see if he can find Max. Pretend it's hide and seek. Buddy is brilliant at that!'

'Of course!' Lauren exclaimed.

'Turn me back into a pony and we can follow him to Max together,' Twilight said.

Lauren looked at Twilight in concern. 'But you're not well. You're too weak.'

'I don't care,' Twilight said, looking determined. 'I want to help you find your brother.'

'Are you sure?' Lauren said.

'Yes,' Twilight insisted. He nudged her with his nose. 'Come on, we're wasting time!'

Lauren didn't argue with him any longer. She turned him back into a pony, then she went into the house to tell her mother her plan, before fetching Buddy.

'We're going to find Max,' she told the

puppy. She saddled Twilight and led him and Buddy to the place where she had last seen Max.

'Find Max, boy,' she said to Buddy. 'Good dog. Off you go.'

Buddy put his nose to the ground and began to snuffle round. Suddenly he seemed to pick up Max's scent. With a woof, he bounded up the path and into the woods. Lauren mounted Twilight and they trotted after him.

Lauren's heart was beating fast as they entered the trees. What if this idea didn't work? What if they all got lost trying to find Max? She pushed the thoughts out of her mind and concentrated on encouraging Buddy.

'That's it!' she called to the puppy.
'Good boy!'

Buddy set off down a narrow trail
away from the main path. Lauren had to
duck under low-hanging branches as the
path twisted and turned. Brambles caught
at her jeans.

She frowned as she tried to work out where they were. They seemed to be heading in the direction of . . .

The gorge!

'Buddy! Be careful!' she gasped in alarm. 'The path ends just ahead. It's dangerous!'

But Buddy started to run even faster. He disappeared from sight.

Lauren wondered what to do, but Twilight took the decision out of her hands. Breaking into a canter, he set off through the trees after the puppy. Lauren flung herself down against his neck. Clinging to Twilight's mane, she looked ahead as best she could.

Suddenly Lauren heard Buddy bark and then Twilight jerked to a stop. Her breath came in short gasps as she pushed herself upright in the saddle. Buddy was just ahead of them. He was standing beside a faded wooden sign that read:

Her heart pounding, Lauren dismounted.

Twilight nuzzled her arm and she could tell he was also worried. Slipping the reins over her arms, she walked cautiously forward. She didn't dare walk right to the edge of the gorge in case the crumbling ground gave way. Letting go of Twilight, she dropped to her hands and knees and crawled the last few metres. She felt sick. What was she going to see when she looked over?

'Buddy!' she called as Buddy inched right to the edge. 'Be careful!'

'Lauren!' a faint voice called.

Lauren felt her heart leap. 'Max!' she gasped.

CHAPTER

Eight

Throwing herself on to her stomach, she looked over the edge of the gorge. Max was crouched on a rocky ledge about four metres below the cliff edge. Beneath him, the gorge tumbled away steeply, ending in a pit of rocks and brambles far, far below. His eyes were wide with fear.

'Lauren,' he cried. 'You found me! I

didn't think anyone ever would.'

'Are you OK?' Lauren asked.

'Yes. I was having a look over the side of the gorge and the ground just sort of crumbled,' Max said. 'But I landed on this ledge. I'm OK. I just can't get back up.'

Lauren went cold as she thought about what might have happened if he hadn't landed on the outcrop.

'I'll go and get help!' she said.

'No! Don't leave me!' Max looked terrified.

Lauren looked desperately at her brother. 'I've got to go. I can't reach you.'

'I don't want to stay here alone,' Max said tearfully.

'But you wouldn't be alone,' Lauren

said desperately. 'Buddy's here.'

'Buddy!' Max gasped in delight. Buddy barked, as if in reply.

'Look, I'm going to have to go and get Mum and Dad, Max,' Lauren said. 'Buddy will stay with you.'

Max looked up. 'OK,' he said bravely.

'I'll be back as soon as I can,' Lauren promised.

Edging away from the cliff, she stood up, commanded Buddy to stay and ran to Twilight. 'Quick, Twilight!' she gasped as she mounted. 'We've got to get home!'

'Lauren! Where have you been? I've been out of mind with worry!' Mrs Foster came running down the path as Lauren

and Twilight galloped out of the woods towards the farm. 'How could you have – ?'

'Mum! I've found Max,' Lauren interrupted her mother as Twilight slowed to a trot. 'He's stuck in the gorge.'

'Oh my goodness,' Mrs Foster said, going pale. 'The gorge!'

'He's all right,' Lauren said. 'He's on a ledge. Buddy's with him.'

'I'll ring your dad,' Mrs Foster said. 'He's in the woods.' She turned and ran back to the house.

'I'll go back there,' Lauren called after her. 'I told Max I'd get back as quickly as I could.'

Mrs Foster stopped. 'OK,' she agreed. 'If you get there before your dad, then

tell Max that help will be along very
soon.' She ran into the house.

'Are you OK to go back, boy?' Lauren
asked Twilight.

He nodded and swung round, pulling
eagerly at his bit. He suddenly seemed
much livelier, almost as if he had got all his
energy back. Lauren leaned forward and
they cantered back into the woods again.

Lauren reached the gorge just as her dad,
Tom and Hank jumped out of the pick-
up truck.

'It's OK, Max,' she said, crawling to the
edge. 'Dad's coming.'

'Thanks for getting help, Lauren,'
murmured her brother.

'Lauren! Thank heavens you found
him!' Mr Foster said, hurrying to the
edge of the gorge. Lying down on his
stomach, he looked over. 'It's all right,
Max,' he said. 'We'll get you up.'

Lauren watched as Tom and Hank tied one end of a long coil of rope securely around a thick oak tree and then, using it to hold on to, her dad lowered himself over the edge.

'We're ready to come back up,' he called, once he had been down there for a few minutes.

There was a bit of shouting and then Tom and Hank began to pull on the rope. Mr Foster and Max soon scrambled over the edge of the gorge.

Lauren sighed with relief as her dad hugged Max as if he were never going to let him go. 'Oh, Max! Why did you go off like that?' he said.

'I'm sorry.' Max looked close to tears

again. 'I was just cross with Lauren. I'm really sorry, Dad.'

Mr Foster hugged him. 'Just don't do anything like it ever again.'

'I won't,' Max said, as Mr Foster put him down. Max looked at Lauren. 'I'm sorry I got upset with you, Lauren.'

'It's OK. I should have let you teach Buddy to fetch,' Lauren told him.

'I was being silly,' Max said. He looked at the ground. 'I'd . . . I'd like you to help me train Buddy if you want.'

Lauren smiled. 'You don't need me. You're doing fine on your own, Max. Anyway, I don't think Buddy needs much training,' she said, looking at the puppy. 'No dog could be cleverer. He

was the one who found you.'

Max crouched down and hugged Buddy. 'Thanks, boy.' Buddy wagged his tail in delight.

'Come on, Max. Let's get you home,' Mr Foster said. 'The pick-up is just through the trees.' He looked at Lauren. 'Will you be OK riding back on your own?'

'I'll be fine,' she said. She waved as her dad, Hank, Tom and Max set off through the shadows. The pick-up started and Lauren listened as it drove away. Once the woods were quiet again, she took off Twilight's bridle and saddle. Then, taking a deep breath, she said the words of the Turning Spell.

Almost before the last word was out
of her mouth, there was a bright purple
flash and Twilight was a unicorn once more.

'Oh, Twilight,' she said, hugging him.
'Thank you for helping me.'

Twilight pushed his nose against her
chest. 'I'm just glad Max is OK,' he said. 'I
wish I could have used my magic to help
you find him more quickly.'

'It doesn't matter now,' Lauren said.
'Your idea to use Buddy was brilliant. If
you hadn't thought of that, Max might
still be stuck. And anyway,' she went on
quickly, 'it wasn't your fault that we
couldn't use magic. It was mine. I was the
one who used it all up by getting you to
look at my friends.'

'You were only trying to help people,'
Twilight reminded her.

'I know,' Lauren said. 'But I didn't
really need magic for that. I could have
seen that Mel was upset about her
fractions and I should have realized that
Jessica was feeling left out, and the other
people I tried to help – Joanne, David,
Max – well, they didn't really need my
help at all.' She looked down. 'I think I
just liked feeling important.'

Twilight nuzzled her. 'Don't feel bad. It
turned out all right in the end.'

'Yes,' Lauren said slowly, 'thanks to you.
You're the best, Twilight. Even though
you were feeling really ill, you still let me
ride you so that we could follow Buddy

here.' She hugged him. 'How are you feeling now?'

Twilight considered the question. 'All right, actually. I don't feel tired at all.'

'Maybe it's because we've just helped Max,' Lauren suggested. 'Perhaps your powers have come back now that we've actually helped someone truly in need like the book said.'

'I'm sure that's what has happened,' Twilight said, tossing his head, 'because I feel great!' He pranced on the spot. 'Let's go flying, Lauren!'

'But it's not dark enough,' Lauren protested.

'I'll stay in the treetops,' Twilight said. He pushed her with his nose. 'Come on!

I want to fly!'

Lauren couldn't resist. 'OK then!' she said, scrambling on to his back.

'I could always use my magic . . .' Twilight began teasingly.

'Not a chance!' Lauren interrupted him with a grin. 'From now on we only use your magic powers to help people who truly need help. Agreed?'

'Agreed,' Twilight said. He started to trot out of the trees and then he stopped. 'Am I really the best?' he asked, almost shyly.

Lauren nodded as she hugged him. 'The very best,' she smiled.

My Secret Unicorn

Flying High

'I wonder what Jessica's doing now,'
she said. 'I wish I knew.'
'Me too,' Twilight said. As he spoke, his
horn touched one of the pink rocks.
There was a bright purple flash.
Twilight shot backwards with a startled
whinny as mist suddenly started to
swirl over the rock.
Lauren leapt to her feet. 'Twilight!'
she gasped.

My Secret Unicorn

Dreams Come True

Mel turned Shadow towards the jump. His
ears pricked up and he quickened his stride.
'He's going to jump it!' Lauren whispered to
Twilight in delight.
Shadow got nearer and nearer, his hooves
thudding on the grass.
Then, a metre in front of the jump, he
suddenly stopped.

My Secret Unicorn

Unicorn

The Magic Spell

Laura tried to imagine her pony. What colour would he be? How old? Maybe he would be a black pony with four white socks, or a flashy chestnut or a snow-white pony with a flowing mane and tail. Lauren smiled to herself. Yes, that's what she'd like – a beautiful white pony.